The
Weight
of Feathers

An anthology of prize-winning short
stories and flash fiction

Edited by
Gaynor Jones

ISBN eBook: 978-1-9196087-2-3
ISBN print: 978-1-9196087-3-0

Retreat West Books
retreatwest.co.uk/books

Contents

Foreword

IT'S SUCH A privilege to be publishing the fifth anthology of stories from the Retreat West Prize. I'm so honoured that writers from all over the world continue to send us their work year after year. It's a pleasure reading it all. Thank you.

Well done to all the writers who submitted a story for the 2020 Prize as it was a difficult year, for creativity and much more, so just getting words on the page was an achievement. Huge congratulations to our winners and shortlisted writers. Getting through to the final ten from the hundreds of entries we receive is no mean feat.

After five years of running the annual prize, this is the final anthology that will feature only short stories and flash fictions as we have added a new category for the 2021 Prize—micro fictions. So the next anthology will have thirty stories instead of twenty and we're delighted to be able to bring even more brilliant writing to readers.

Many thanks to Peter Jordan and Susmita Bhattacharya for judging the 2020 prize and choosing the winners in the Short Story and Flash Fiction category, respectively. I am always glad to hand over this final decision as by the time we have reached the shortlist, all of the stories that have made it through have earned a special place in my heart. Thanks also to Louise Walters who helps me read for the Prizes and choose the long and shortlists. I couldn't do it without you, and it would be a lot less fun if I did!

I hope everyone who reads this anthology enjoys these brilliant stories as much as we do.

Amanda Saint

Short Story Judge's Report – Peter Jordan

FIRST PRIZE: THE STONECUTTER'S MASTERPIECE BY JENNIFER FALKNER

Peter said: I read each story in a single day; one after the other, then slept on it. But I have to say I had a firm idea which story was the best from the first read. The next day, I read the ten stories again and the winning story survived and passed the second read, and it also survived days of reflection. *The Stonemason's Masterpiece* was an easy choice. The idea of having a woman made of stone seek a stone-cutter for release was superb. But it wasn't the idea that won it. Ideas don't win writing comps. It won because the writing on an individual sentence level was superb.

SECOND PRIZE: DANIEL SPRINKLES STARS BY HOLLY BARRATT

Peter said: All good stories have a surface story, with something understated—often bigger than the surface story—running underneath. The is the case with *Daniel Sprinkles Stars*. And the writing is controlled, and consistently in the voice of the central character, Daniel.

THIRD PRIZE: BOOBOO BY JOHN HOLLAND

Peter said: I chose *Booboo* because the story is possibly the simplest with regards to both prose and story. In many ways *Booboo* is the perfect template for a short story. Start late, leave early. Keep it simple. Have the surface story allude to bigger things—in this case, the mother's new partner and how that affects her young daughter.

Short Story First Prize

The Stonecutter's Masterpiece

Jennifer Falkner

WHEN SHE APPEARED, a half-veiled figure slowly coming down the road, he thought she came with a commission. No one else ever came down into this valley. His workshop was the only thing in it, curled at the bottom of it like a sleeping cat.

As she came closer, the stonecutter saw she wasn't veiled at all, just wrapped sensibly against the cold. She wore a scarf over her hair, a plain mackintosh, an ankle-length wool skirt. Her hands were gloved and she wore heavy, sensible shoes, which dragged and drew grooves in the gravel road as she walked. The only part of her that remained uncovered was her face, which was pale and finely lined.

He took in her eyes bruised by tiredness, the slight hunch. She was younger than he was, late forties perhaps, early fifties. Patience on a monument, he thought. He gestured to the only seat, a white plastic lawn chair, and offered tea from his flask. There was a grinding sound, like mortar against pestle, as she lowered herself down.

'We've met before.' Her accent was foreign, vaguely Scottish. It was pleasing, the way it tumbled gently around her mouth like pebbles down a rock slip. 'You replaced one of the gargoyles on our battlements. Ashworth House.'

That had been a good job, taking him away from Pembrokeshire and the gravestones that were his bread and butter. They required no skill beyond spelling the departed's name correctly. Plus, the National Trust had paid surprisingly well.

'Mrs Adams, isn't it?'

'Yes.'

'Another shaky gargoyle?'

She cupped the mug of tea in her fingers, but didn't lift it to her lips.

'I'm not a trustee anymore. I've retired.' She paused and looked around, as if gathering in her next words from the workshop around her, the rubble on the ground, the chisels and mallets lying on the wooden table, the raised garage door exposing them to the elements.

'Do you need to see the shape in the stone before you start chipping away at it? Does the stone tell you what it is, what it wants to be?' she said.

She spoke with such directness, yet the stonecutter couldn't guess at her real meaning. He leaned against the workbench, wishing he had more than one chair. He wasn't used to visitors.

'That's not how it works,' he said. 'You have to work from a model. I sculpt the subject first in clay.' He talked as if this was something he still did, as if he were still a sculptor, an artist, not just the local stonemason. It felt good to talk this way.

Strands of steam danced up from her tea, blurring her features. 'Couldn't you shorten the process by going to the stone first and last?'

There was something about the determined way she asked, like someone with a stutter forcing the words out. As if his answer would mean everything to her. He shrugged. 'It's possible.'

'I really didn't know who else to ask.'

She handed the mug back to him just as a gust of wind blew through the valley. It lifted her skirt slightly and he glimpsed, above her shoe, the coarse grain of granite.

It had started with her feet, she told him. With cracks in her heels that she thought were just dry skin. A vaguely greyish tone that she thought was a sign of poor circulation. Rock dust in her sheets when she woke in the morning. Freckles on her arms that shimmered like grains of quartz. Then her knees started to grow lumpen, inelegant, bending her legs in unnatural angles, grinding with every movement. She lifted her skirt to show him. She'd had such nice legs, before, she said. Strong legs.

'Can you help me?'

***

BEFORE HE ACCEPTED, he would have to see her. All of her. That was his condition. He would never accept a delivery from a quarry without inspecting it first.

The wind blew through the valley again and with it a cold spattering of rain. Automatically he started putting away his tools, protecting them from moisture and rust. In movements almost as automatic, she began to undress. There was that sound again, the grinding of mortar and pestle. Her movements were slow, laboured, but she displayed no sign of shame or embarrassment or even cold. When he turned back around, there she was.

'This is not really me,' she said. 'It's more like – a shell.'

She was a woman assembled from boulders. The hair on her head grew in patches; in places where she was bald, skin had turned to rock. Unmoving breasts overhung a cold, grey belly. Thighs that were practically egg-shaped showed signs of erosion where they rubbed together.

'Every day I change a little more.'

He reached out. 'Do you mind –' but he didn't wait for an answer. His hands were on her, feeling the rock, sliding over its surface, sometimes smooth, sometimes pitted. He was measuring her with his fingers first, before he brought out the calipers. Learning her. She was something between a bluestone and something much softer, like marble, he thought. She was like nothing he had seen before. Mrs Adams fixed her gaze on the horizon.

The stonecutter dropped his hands from her body. There were spots of rain on his glasses and his breath released small puffs of fog between them. He nodded slowly. He folded his arms, took a step back and nodded again. It must also have been rain that wetted her cheeks.

'When do you want to start?' he said.

***

THE PROJECT EXCITED him, he couldn't deny it. It brought back that rush of feeling he remembered from his long-ago twenties, when he had first toured the marble workshops of Florence and Rome. When his ambition still surpassed his skill and nothing surpassed his expectations.

He didn't even bother with the point chisel since the general shape was already there. He had visions of the Nike of Samothrace, how its ancient carver had created delicate folds of fabric, gauze out of rock, that fluttered and moved and revealed the body beneath. He started with a flat chisel. The stonecutter could see, emerging beneath his hands, the delicate weave of cloth, the smoothness of thigh.

There was a dry rumble that might have been a groan.

'Are you all right?'

'I'm fine.' Her voice sounded like it was coming from far away, yet he could feel the vibration of it in the cool rock beneath his hands. 'It's fine.'

'Do you want me to stop?'

'No. It only hurts a little. Go on. Go on.'

He proceeded more slowly. He tried to be gentle, but how can you chisel and crack and chip away gently? His chisel sang against the stone, as clear and light as a bell.

She stood straight, arms at her sides like a caryatid or one of those simple Egyptian funerary statues. But he would cut movement into her. Her clothes would blow against her body, her face would tilt upwards and give a Mona Lisa-like smile to the sky. He had in mind something classical. A vaguely toga-like garment. Leather sandals on her bare feet. She might adorn a pagan temple.

It could take weeks, months perhaps. He set up several work lights to extend his working hours. He felt guilty when he stopped to rest, to sleep in the cot he kept in the back of the workshop or to have a bite of something, while she stood motionless outside. Within days her metamorphosis was complete and she was all stone. Movement was impossible. Her gaze was fixed upwards, as if she was an augur and, having mapped out the sky, was waiting for a message to fly across it. He could hear gulls sometimes – they weren't that far from the sea – and ravens, though he rarely saw them.

They talked as he worked. Though her lips and jaw had hardened into stone, her voice floated through his mind. He smoothed away the corrugations made by his toothed chisel, the grooves in her forehead, the wrinkles in front of her ears, and his rasp against the stone sometimes sounded like a whisper. He found himself telling her about the long-ago years of his apprenticeship, about the first time he saw Canova's Cupid and Psyche and what a revelation that was. He travelled back over years. And beneath his hands she grew younger too. Her hair was now gathered in tendrils along her neck, her dress in folds beneath her breasts, along her hips. He was no Phidias, but he wasn't bad. He could make something that would last. She helped him believe in himself again.

Christmas came and he draped gold tinsel over her shoulders and toasted her with rum and eggnog. At her request, he played carols on his small radio. The sound was terrible, tinny and small, but she didn't seem to mind. She hummed along in his mind. Her voice was deeper, more resonant than he remembered. She liked the old carols, *The Holly and the Ivy, Greensleeves.*

But after Christmas she spoke less and less. It was the beginning of February when he finished; he'd almost forgotten the feel of her voice floating through his head.

The stonecutter brought a full-length mirror from his apartment. She was a Greek goddess, ageless and beautiful. Her wrinkles were gone, her hunch smoothed away. He felt silly holding the mirror up to a statue, asking what it thought.

Silence at first. And then a small voice, like the finest grade of sandpaper. *This is not me.* It repeated it. *This is not me.* And grew louder, rising to the roar of an avalanche. *This is not what I meant at all!*

'Oh, isn't it?' the stonecutter growled. He had poured months of work into this, he had turned down paying commissions to complete this, what he knew was his masterpiece, his highest achievement. He hurled the mirror to the ground. It smashed against the concrete floor, but it was not destruction enough. All that work, months and months, the utmost of his skill. Whoever heard of carving a life-size statue without even using a plaster model? He did not get it wrong.

The stonecutter snatched up a hammer and chisel from his tool bench. The nose came off with one hit. The ears too, and the graceful fingers. Whack, whack, whack. His chisel didn't sing against the stone, it stuttered. It raged. He gouged out chunks from her head, her torso, circling and pounding at random. His beloved drapery crumbled.

When he had finished, when he fell to his knees amid the rubble, pink-faced and panting, she was no longer a woman. Certainly not the most beautiful figure he had ever carved. A blocky head, a vague torso, still oddly supported by perfectly chiselled sandaled feet. Barely human.

Show me.

He raised his face from his hands. 'What?'

Show me. The voice was urgent.

He picked a long mirror shard, careful of its sharp edges.

Yessss, she sighed. *Finally.*

Lumpen and disfigured. He couldn't bear to dwell on the result of his destruction. Where the chisel had broken pieces away, its inner porphyritic texture was revealed, rough and uneven, in all the colours of the earth. He looked away.

'You look like a ruin.'

Finally, she said in his mind, *I look like myself.*

***

IT WAS THE last thing she ever said to him.

He walked carefully around her, avoiding her gaze as he cleaned his tools and swept the floor. Eventually he grew tired of attempting awkward, one-sided conversations. Of half-apologies. And after a while, after many days, he even began to wonder if he had only ever imagined her voice, her original commission. The whole thing was absurd. Distasteful.

Her presence filled him with shame.

He had a girlfriend from Canada once, an arctic researcher, and he lived with her in Nunavut for one sunless winter. It was there he first saw a real inuksuk. Not one of those kitschy fiberglass things people put in their gardens. It was only about four feet tall, a figure of a man made by piling rocks together. Its arms stuck straight out, like a child's drawing of a stick figure, but with one arm much longer than the other. She told him it was indicating the direction to the nearest settlement. He never forgot that. That empty land, draped in cold, populated by stone people pointing the way home.

The stonecutter draped her in blue padded blankets, tied them around with thin, yellow rope for the journey. She was almost too heavy for him to manage on his own. He heaved and pushed and grunted and tipped her onto the dolly, then into his truck. He was thankful for the violent hewing he had done, the removal of that extra weight was necessary for him to get her even this far. He drove out of his valley, from which he'd always had to look up to see the horizon, and headed for the Preseli hills.

***

HE UNTIED THE ropes, pulled the blankets away in a flourish. She still looked terrible, like something that had erupted from the raw earth. He turned her. Turned her again, one more inch, so she might face west, the direction of the sea. Her quartz-freckled body glinted in the sunlight. Her sandaled feet flattened the grass and dug into the ground. There were others like her here, standing stones. She would not be alone.

He hoped she would say something, some word of acknowledgement, of farewell. He hoped he'd hear something beyond the sound of the wind and the gulls crying overhead. He wanted to know he had done the right thing.

The stonecutter climbed back into his truck. He thought, with regret, of her finely-lined eyes. Of his now-empty workshop.

Overhead, the sky changed and changed.

Short Story Second Prize

Daniel Sprinkles Stars

Holly Barratt

DADDY PUTS ON music.

He flicks through playlists on the tablet and eventually decides he'll listen to something loud with no words.

'What's this music Daddy?'

'Vivaldi. Come into the kitchen a moment Daniel.'

Daddy hasn't listened to any music for a few weeks now. Instead they have the live feed from the Artemis mission on a screen in every room except the bathroom and the kitchen. Daniel has to watch his cartoons on an old tablet on his lap. Sometimes the feed is silent and dark for hours, just a little fleck of light now and then from a distant star. Sometimes there is a low buzz, like an old fridge, or a squealing sound that Daniel can hear but Daddy can't – they looked it up on the internet and it turned out that old people couldn't hear it because of the frequency.

Daddy thought that was interesting and kept asking

whether Daniel could hear anything whenever he couldn't. Which was most of the time.

Today the screen on the living room is switched off. Daniel doesn't mind much. Although it does make the room seem quiet, even though the screen is normally silent and today there's Vivaldi.

Daddy takes Daniel's hand and touches his chin.

'Would you like to make a cake?'

Daddy has a cut on his face. The blood is splodged over his chin, and there's another splodge on the collar of his t-shirt. His t-shirt says 'physicists do it at the speed of light' – but it doesn't say what they do. Daddy does physics. Mummy does too. Neither of them makes cakes very often and it's not even his birthday.

'Can it be a space cake? Steffan had a space cake at his birthday party.'

'Yes. It can be a space cake.'

Daddy's voice is a bit strange. Maybe he has a sore throat.

'Can we look at the Artemis feed and copy the space we can see?'

'Maybe later. We need to bake the cake first.'

Daniel starts thinking about the Artemis feed again. Sometimes when it's not dark and quiet, it's bright and light with little clouds – like a day on earth. Daniel was surprised because he thought space was always dark, but now he understands that space can be all different colours.

Sometimes, especially after a few weeks into the mission, it was swirls of purple, like blueberry milkshake. Sometimes it flashed brightly in one colour or all different colours. Sometimes a planet, or part of one, would roll past for a few days, changing colour all the time. Sometimes the feed would look like the night sky on earth, full of tiny little sparkling stars.

Daniel thinks he would like part of the cake to be like swirling milkshake, and part of it to be dark blue with little stars. And with a big silver model of the Artemis in the middle. That would make it better than Steffan's – he only had a pretend spaceship. Not a real one. But Steffan's Mummy works in an office, so she might not know what a real spaceship looks like.

'Can I bring my Artemis model down Daddy? So we can copy it for the cake?'

'Later. Come on, we're going to weigh things for the recipe now.'

Daddy gets the scales down from on top of the cupboard and wipes off the dust with a tea towel. He shows Daniel the numbers in the recipe book and pours flour into the dish of the scales.

'See, 300 grams?'

Daniel nods and Daddy pours the flour into the bowl.

'Now we weigh the sugar.'

Daddy looks at his phone then quickly puts it back in his pocket. It's 2.38pm. On a Sunday afternoon, if the feed is on, the cameras turn inside the Artemis for a few hours and you can see the crew. Usually they are just cleaning or moving things around. Then one or two of them go into the diary room and they talk to everyone watching about what they've been doing that week. Ryan does experiments in the lab. Elsa and Lewis fly the ship. Dylan fixes anything that goes wrong. Mummy watches space and takes measurements. People love to hear Mummy talk the most of all. She talks about all of the amazing planets and stars they've seen, and how beautiful the galaxy is, and how strange the measurements she's taking are. Around 3pm, Mummy calls Daddy and Daniel to talk just to them. She usually only talks about stars and measurements a little bit, but then she talks about what Daniel has been doing at school, and whether he's being good, and how Daddy's work is, and if he's remembering to take his vitamin tablets.

If they spend too long in the kitchen making the cake they might miss Mummy's call.

'Now we put the sugar in this bowl. And we put the butter in too, and we have to whisk it.'

Daddy looks around the kitchen and opens and shuts a few drawers, each one louder than the last.

'OK. No whisk. It's fine, we can use this fork. It'll be fine.'

Daddy stirs the butter and sugar very quickly. Some of it gathers together in a big lump, but a lot of it flies out of the bowl and lands on Daddy's t-shirt and in Daniel's hair.

'Daddy!'

'Sorry. Sorry. You have a go. Gently does it. Like this.'

Daniel seems to be better than Daddy at whisking butter and sugar – it starts to look like mashed potato.

Daddy looks at the book for a long time before he says

'Now we add the butter and sugar to the flour and baking soda.'

Daddy scrapes the butter and sugar into the big bowl with the flour and mixes it all together before pouring it into a big black metal tin and putting it in the oven. He looks at his phone again.

'25 minutes Daniel. Do you want me to find you a cartoon?'

'Can we talk to Mummy?'

Daddy looks out of the window into the garden. It's just started raining.

'I – um. Well, why not watch a cartoon now, and perhaps we'll be able to talk to Mummy once the cake is done?'

'I can show her the decorations and the stars and the spaceship.'

'I hope so yes. That'd be great, wouldn't it?'

Daddy hands Daniel the tablet with a boring cartoon about rabbits on it. He can't even hear it properly because the Vivaldi is still playing. But then Daddy goes into the bathroom for a long time so Daniel has to carry on watching it because he doesn't know how to work the old tablet.

Daddy comes out of the bathroom and pulls Daniel towards him for a big hug. Daniel's nose gets turned up like a pig nose as it squashes against a bone in Daddy's hip.

'You're squishing me!'

Daddy lets go and sighs.

'Shall we decorate the cake then?'

Daddy opens the oven and makes a face when a cloud of steam hits him. He uses a tea towel to protect his hands and lifts the cake out onto the side. Then he takes lots of things out of a cupboard and puts them next to the cake – a cheese grater, the fizzy drink making machine that Mummy bought once but they never really used, a big bowl with some foreign writing on it that came from somewhere Mummy and Daddy went before Daniel was born, and some dirty looking egg cups that Daniel doesn't remember seeing ever before. Then Daddy takes out an old ice-cream tub, that has some little bottles of food colouring and some jars of sprinkles. Daniel remembers them from his birthday. He remembers there are silver stars.

Daddy pours icing sugar into a bowl, then adds some water from the filter until it goes wet and sticky. He divides the mixture into two bowls and lets Daniel choose the colours. Daniel chooses dark blue and purple. Daddy even lets Daniel add the colour himself, but he thinks he's added too much purple, because that bowl is so dark it's almost black. Like when the Artemis feed is really boring.

Daddy uses a knife to spread the icing on two sides of the cake – blue one side, purple black the other. He is quite messy, and the icing keeps soaking into the cake and running down the sides so they need to use a lot.

When he's done, Daniel sprinkles the stars over the top. Lots and lots, like a starry night on earth and in space.

'Can we make an Artemis now Daddy?'

'We need to wait for the icing to dry first I think.'

'But how long will that take? We won't be able to show Mummy!'

Daniel can see the clock on Daddy's phone as he takes it out of his pocket again. It is already after 4 o'clock.

'It doesn't matter Daniel!' Daddy sounds like he's trying to shout but he's too quiet. His throat must be really sore. Then he goes into the bathroom again and slams the door.

Daniel thinks it does matter. Daddy doesn't make cakes very often, and this one won't last until next Sunday. He wants to talk to Mummy anyway. Even if they don't finish the cake.

The Vivaldi music stops, and Daniel can hear Daddy

talking behind the bathroom door. His voice is so low and the door so thick that he can't hear the words, but he must be on the phone. Which means Daddy is on the phone to Mummy without him. Maybe Daddy thinks the cake is too messy to show Mummy. Maybe he thought he wouldn't make a good Artemis model, so he didn't want to show her. Daddy is silly and annoying.

Daniel wants to see Mummy. He walks over to the screen in the living room and presses the button that Daddy always presses.

The screen comes on, but it's not Mummy. Not Ryan or Elsa or the others either. And it's not purple or blue or full of stars – it's just a black screen with some white writing on it. Daniel recognises some of the letters but he doesn't know what it says. He'll need Daddy to read it to him when he comes out of the bathroom.

Daniel waits by the bathroom door.

He hears Daddy shouting for a minute. Then he goes quiet

'Daddy?'

Daddy doesn't answer

Daniel goes back to the kitchen and looks at all the stars he's sprinkled. The icing is running and some of the stars are dragged with it, leaving little silver tails like meteoroids. It's still a good cake. He really hopes he'll be able to make a good Artemis model to put on top and show Mummy.

Short Story Prize Third Prize

Booboo

John Holland

WHO THOUGHT THIS was a good idea? A night-time owl flying display—in the open air. Mum obviously thinks so because she's brought me, her beloved daughter, with her. And him, of course.

In my experience night does have a tendency to be dark so what're we going to see? To be fair, there are a few dim lights, and they've got the biggest owl in town. It's an Eagle Owl—like a cross between an owl and an eagle. It's massive. There are gasps when the man walks with the owl on his arm into the display area. And those eyes—two enormous yellow globes at the front of its head.

We're all sitting on wooden benches in the dark, about thirty of us, all muffled in our big coats against the cold. It's like bonfire night except without the heat and the fun.

'Booboo,' announces the man, 'is a female—females are bigger than males. She has a three metre wingspan.

Show them your wings, Booboo. Come on, girl.'

Booboo complies, unfolding and stretching wings that are so huge you could use them as a tent, or maybe the roof of a small house. She creates a draft so strong that people are holding onto their children to stop them lifting into the air.

The man is wearing big leather gloves to protect his hand from the owl's talons, which are like hunting knives.

We're sitting in the front row—Mum and me and Mum's 'friend' whose name is 'Alan'. I can barely bring myself to say it. Obviously Mum is sitting between 'Alan' and me. He's feeding Mum mints and keeps leaning across with his minty breath to offer one to me, but, each time, I don't take one. I want to say, 'Look, there's a trend emerging here, fuckwit—I'm not taking anything from you.' But I just shake my head.

Mum is being too nice, saying how lovely I look and asking if I'm enjoying myself, which is making me feel nauseous.

The man takes the Eagle Owl into this small dark field in front of us. Puts it on top of a wooden pole, and walks about twenty yards away from it. Even sitting in the front row it's hard to make out the owl.

He announces, like he's a male version of God, 'Let there be light.' Great columns of silver rise from hidden floodlights in the ground. They stream into the night sky. Like in a film about London in the blitz. The crowd goes

'Oooo.' The owl blinks.

The god-man calls out, 'Booboo, Booboo,' and the owl flies low over the ground like a Stealth Bomber, illuminated by the beams of white light, before landing with its huge claws on his gloved hand.

He does this a couple of times before asking if anyone would like to have a go. People look at each other, and 'Alan' leans over Mum and actually touches my arm with his repulsive hand and says, 'How about you, Tara?'

Mum says, 'Go on, love.'

The god-man sees us and calls out, 'Yes, young lady, how about it?' I'm rooted to the spot and say, 'No thank you.' And think, you won't get me near that monster.

A hefty black-haired woman in a tight leopard-skin coat sticks her hand in the air, straining her arm upwards as if she's a kid in class.

'Anyone else?' the god-man says, obviously not keen on the bloated leopard woman.

But with no other takers, he says, 'Ok, my love,' encouraging the leopard-woman to step forward. He walks the Eagle Owl back to its post and returns to stand next to the woman. He fits one of her hands with a leather glove.

'Do you have insurance?' he asks her, in a tone that means he's joking. She doesn't smile, but some of the audience laugh.

'Is that your husband over there?' he asks her.

'No,' she says, 'it's my fella.'

'Well, just take a moment to wave goodbye to him.' Even though it's a joke she actually does wave. Her fella doesn't wave back.

'I'm joking,' he says. If only, I think.

He presses something red and squidgy into her gloved hand. 'Now, hold out your hand for Booboo. No, not that one, the one with the glove and the meat.' She does this stiffly like her arm is made of metal.

'Booboo,' he shouts. 'Are you ready, girl?'

The great owl takes off from its post and flies, but not to the woman, instead directly towards the audience. I feel its massive wings like a rush of blood to the head as it swoops over me. For that second it is how I imagine it is to be taken into the belly of a whale or sent into space in a rocket. At that moment I belong to the owl. There's another 'Ooooo' from the crowd. But instead of flying back to the leopard-woman, it soars silently into the bough of a huge tree behind us.

The bald man in the row behind me rubs his head, and I imagine the great owl's huge talons gashing his naked scalp. Five red lines of ripped flesh oozing blood.

'Don't worry,' the god-man says. 'That's her favourite tree. Let's call her again.'

And he does. 'Din dins, Booboo.' And then he makes the leopard-woman call too.

By the eighth time he's called 'din dins' he has asked

the leopard-woman to sit down and is standing under the tree holding a piece of red meat in the air. I imagine the owl swooping down and ripping off his arm then returning to the tree to gnaw on it. But the owl just sits there making a contented bubbling sound, her head constantly swivelling, looking everywhere except at the man. I can feel how much happier she is, out of the limelight, with no pressure to behave or please anyone. I am willing her to fly into the night sky.

The crowd is getting restless and the man is making his excuses. 'She did have quite a large lunch today.' His tone is becoming increasingly strained.

'Eagle owls are, of course, wild creatures with minds of their own. She'd prefer to take live food. In the forest they might sit silently until a rabbit, a hare or even a fox, came within striking distance. Then wallop!'

There's not a lot of walloping going on here, so people in the audience start making helpful suggestions.

'Can't you get a ladder, mate?'

Of course 'Alan' has to shout something. 'Try him with one of my Butter Mints, pal.'

Mum laughs the oddest laugh I've ever heard. Like a parrot being strangled underwater.

Someone shouts, 'Aven't you got another owl you can show us?'

'Not really,' he says, looking like he might cry.

People start to wander off. 'Can we have our money

back, mate?'

He's begging the bird. 'Booboo, please come and eat your dins dins for the ladies and gentlemen.'

'Perhaps she's a vegetarian,' someone says.

'Come down here or you're in big trouble, girl.' The man's tone has changed.

But the bird ignores him, still making that throaty bubbling sound. More people start wandering off.

'Yes, yes,' the man says, 'do enquire at the office for a refund.'

Mum and 'Alan' decide to leave and ask if I'm coming.

'I'll wait a bit longer,' I say.

'Suit yourself,' Mum says. 'See you in the car park.'

'Yeah, don't be long or we might be in the back seat, you know what I'm saying?' snorts 'Alan'. I watch them walk off hand-in-hand. I feel a small amount of vomit rise in my throat.

The man is now at the top of a ladder, which, even with his arm outstretched, doesn't extend to the owl. He's still holding the meat. I am still willing her to fly.

'Go on, girl,' I hear myself say.

As I watch, the owl nonchalantly leans forward and takes to the wing. I can feel a gust of air—even where I'm sitting. The ladder falls from under the man's feet. He grabs a branch and gains some footing on a bough. It's like a scene from a silent movie. The owl flies to another tree on the edge of the car park.

As I walk back to the car park I pause beneath the tree where the owl is. I shout into the high branches 'Booboo, Booboo'—like the crazy owner of a tree-climbing dog.

I imagine her flying down to me and landing on my shoulder, her talons through my overcoat, their tips piercing my skin, her feathers smelling of the forest, of wildness, of raw life.

Then I see her. She's taken to the air, her great wings outstretched, her huge form disappearing into the night. I stare for a few minutes into the blue-black sky, before walking to the car where Mum and 'Alan' are waiting.

I don't share with them what I have seen. That she has flown and is free. And on the journey home I don't speak. I just peer from inside the car into the beckoning darkness.

Words

Jane Fraser

I LOVE WORDS. Always have. Words are my job – I'm a teacher of linguistics. When I was young and my name was Evelyn Foster, I would list the words I loved most in a feint-lined pocket notebook with a red cover. Diligently, I would add new words to the list as they thrilled me with their sound – usually on a weekly basis: neatly; in block capitals; word on the left and the reason why I liked them on the right. It looked something like this:

Words I like most by Evelyn Foster aged 11.

LULLABY	I like the gentle sound. I think it's the l. It is a sleepy word.
SIGH	This is a soft word, it hardly makes a sound.
GOSSAMER	We had this word in a poem at school, I don't remember what it means but it sounds light and weightless. The m is a nice sound, airless, tickles the lips.

MELLIFLUOUS   We had this in a poem by John Keats –
it was in a phrase the mellifluous haunt
of flies of summer eves and Mr. Ware
told us that the words actually *sounded*
like the noise the flies make – I can't
remember the word he used, on a mat
or something, but it was very clever.

This, I suppose, was the time I began to realise that the sounds of words could help re-enforce meaning, or semantics, as they say in our profession. Or perhaps I should say as *I* say in *my* profession. Though I've tended not to say much these last few years that uses the personal or possessive pronoun. Strange for someone in my line of work who loves words so much.

I still write though, as I used to, in a little spiral-bound exercise book which I squirrel away in my bedside drawer. I'm still a stickler for recording words and phrases that are memorable, that strike me for some reason or other. I use the same basic template; word or phrase or utterance (not sentence – we are talking here, spoken not written language) on the left and a brief description of my personal response on the right. It looks something like this:

Memorable words & phrases by Evelyn Francis* age 51
(I forgot, this book has a black cover.)

CLAP TRAP	Memorable. One syllable. Punchy. Repetition of phonetic /aep/
FLAPPING YOUR LIPS	Hate this. Images of birds. When accompanied by hand action, in close up, it is terrifying.
SHUT THE FUCK UP	Menacing. Keeps repeating in my head. Anglo-Saxon monosyllabic word.
KEEP YOUR GOB SHUT AND YOUR LEGS OPEN	Use of the declarative – always so many commands.
WHO NEEDS A DEGREE WHEN THERE'S THE UNIVERSITY OF LIFE?	Yes, the eternal chip on the shoulder.
A GOOD KICKING	Implies repeated action, a series of kicks, becomes a collective noun.
A PUNCH IN THE GOB	Onomatopoeic and monosyllabic.

ON AND ON
AND ON AND ON   Hypnotic chain of
lexis………..how long? My
God, how long?

*sometimes I think that my mother might have been right with her little rhyme:

> *Change the name and not the letter*
> *Change for worse and not for better*

I trust you get the gist. My recorded writing tends to be less regimented and more *ad hoc,* as they say. I write as and when an event occurs – sometimes daily, sometimes weekly. Sometimes I'll go for a few weeks without the need to record. But this is most unusual. I find this way I can create more immediacy and attempt to make more sense of things.

If someone somewhere, an outsider, were to analyse these books, I think it would be relatively simple to draw some conclusions linguistically. I often recast my professional eye – expert and objective – over my childhood lists of vocabulary. Literary, multi-syllabic, often Latinate, often poetic. I then analyse the vocabulary I am immersed in forty years on. Non-literary, colloquial, vernacular, often clichéd platitudes and collocations, simple lexis, mostly single syllables, use of onomatopoeia (that was the word I couldn't recall in childhood but I know it now) predominant use of Anglo-Saxon lexis especially for action words, doing words, verbs such as punch, kick, slap, split.

I would assume the analyst would pose the question, 'What does this language tell us about the speaker's gender? Ethnicity? Social class? Attitudes and Values?' I would be able to say quite a bit, I feel on that subject about these people. I would go so far as to say I would be able to write up a substantial report based on my suppositions and conclusions. I would be able to draw a lot of inferences about the speaker – on paper at least. I might even form opinions, judgments, pointers for action, the range of desirable outcomes that objective professionals make. For I have to keep telling myself, I am, after all, a professional.

I have friends who are high functioning alcoholics: I'm in good company, and I believe I still function like the best of them, at least I have done until now. No-one outside these four walls would ever know – not even my Mother and Father. To them I'm still their little girl who has everything, a good-looking husband with his own business, my own profession, two beautiful children, two granddaughters, a home in the country, the Labrador dog, the pewter Aga. I was the first person they knew to have a built-in waste-disposer and a self-cleaning oven. What would they think if they'd known I'd sold my soul for a Mercedes Benz? *Domestic Violence is no respecter of income, you know*, I feel like screaming, *or social class.* But of course, I don't. I am dumb to tell them. My voice is no longer even a whisper. But I have my black book.

Back in the late seventies when I was in my twenties, there was a song by Billy Joel called, *She's Always a Woman*, which he'd keyed into. He had a terrible voice but he'd always sing it to me. So perhaps there was a time when there was love. Though there was always the ugly spectre of fear and insecurity and I mistook power and control for love.

And already by the early eighties, by the time we'd had our third fitted kitchen put in, he was telling me quite rationally how they'd never find my body. I remember distinctly as it was the brand spanking-new kitchen appliances that acted as the catalyst for what he deemed very creative thinking:

the waste disposer This was cutting edge and plumbed into the sink. It enabled food waste – bones, vegetable skins, fats – to be stuffed into the large aperture in the sink with a plunger and then ground down with the blade mechanisms in the steel body of the machine. The residue would simply drain away with the water without trace…

| **the self-cleaning oven** | This was a fan-assisted double-oven with the great advantage of no cleaning. You simply set the dial to self-clean and the oven would heat to the intensity of an inferno. Any food residue that was in the oven would be burnt to cinders. All that would remain was a small heap of fine white dust which could be wiped away in a simple flick with a damp cloth… |

His other *wheeze,* as he used to call it, to dispose of me, was just not worth bothering about after the kitchen appliances had been installed. Boring and predictable for someone to accidently fall off a narrow cliff path when out for a walk with the husband and the dog, wasn't it? I have to say, I agreed with him. It was always best to agree.

Recently, my daughter had a waste disposer and a fan-assisted oven installed in her swish house in Fulham. Coincidentally they are *Neff* too and when I heard the grinding of the motor and the whirring of the fan over the Christmas period, I felt suddenly sick and shut myself in their downstairs cloakroom, retching violently into the lavatory. I felt outside myself in a way I've never felt before, a spectator observing a play. Perhaps it was the time of year that brought about a feeling of not being myself at all.

She asked me to stay on a while into the New Year. Why not? I thought, I didn't have to be back in school until the 12ᵗʰ January. So *he* went home. People depended on him, he said, the world didn't stop turning in business like it did in education. And he gave me one of those looks, the look with the muscle twitch under the left eye. I didn't say anything. But I stayed.

It was when I went to the bedroom that I really started to feel peculiar – cold and clammy, vibrations running down my legs and in my stomach. It was almost as though a big black bird with enormous wings was flapping inside my body, beating my skin from the inside out. I tried to take deep breaths the way I had through the years when I felt I was losing control, before I could get to my little black book. But it wasn't working. My breath was coming in spasms and I felt dizzy. There was a metallic taste in my mouth, the way I'd have before my periods when I was younger. I needed my book. Record words. Make calm out of chaos, this scene of mid-life tragedy that was playing out before me in my daughter's bedroom with floor-to-ceiling mirrors on the wardrobe doors.

And that's when I saw her, looking at me from the mirror. She was waving at me, her hands gesturing me towards the glass. She was trying to say something, but the sound was muffled, indistinct. Instinctively, I drew towards her. I recognised her, though she'd changed so much in the intervening years. The dark curly hair was long gone, replaced with hair half-brown, half-white. A woman in transition. The eyes were somehow sadder and the sadness brought about an almost convulsive sob, primitive and animal; a lone sob in a frightening world. I thought of those eyes as they'd been, alive with possibility and enquiry. The eyes of the girl who was always smiling. The girl who never stopped talking.

I sat on the edge of the bed and stretched out my hands, fingertip to fingertip with the girl in the glass. She struggled to talk, but she persisted in trying. Face to face we were then, close-up, and I could see, and smell, adhesive. It was caked along her lips, congealed in globules at the corners of her mouth. I knew it was *Bostik* at once, for when my daughter was a tiny girl, and I'd been cleaning out drawers, she'd put a tube of it in her mouth and chewed. She'd bitten through the tube and the glue had stuck fast. In terror, I'd taken her to A & E. It was the fear, always the fear. They'd take my children away. The Social Workers. I was an unfit parent. He'd never let me have my kids. What good would I be to anyone without him? I'd go crawling back. What was I without him? I would be nothing. It must have been at that *Bostik* moment that I began losing my voice.

I dipped gently into the reflection. With my index

finger, I began picking the glue away from her top lip with my nail. I delved into both corners and scraped a little harder. I could feel the warmth of her breath and at the same time, could feel an itching sensation in my own mouth. I worked on, prizing her lips wider to reveal the teeth, the tongue, allowing the hidden mechanics of the mouth freedom. Her lips parted and the sounds she uttered became audible. The larynx, the vocal chords, the mouth's inner chamber all began to work together. *Where did you go?* she shouted, *where did you go?*

Her anger was disconcerting, but perfectly justified, I reasoned. I'd let myself down, perhaps all women down, for reasons only I would ever know. For an intelligent woman I'd made some very unwise decisions in my fifty-one years. I stood up and stared full-on at the girl in the mirror. *I'm still here,* I whispered and then a little louder, *I'm still here.* She said nothing but smiled and gave me the thumbs-up. I still couldn't find my book, but I wasn't in a state about it at all. I grabbed one of the grandchildren's magic markers, a big fat red one and scrawled over the clear glass mirror in bold, upper-case I'M STILL HERE AND I'VE FOUND MY VOICE !!!! with not one, but four exclamation marks which professionally, I'd normally hate for two reasons. Firstly, the over-zealous use of this punctuation device and secondly, because it's simply such bad grammar to use four rather than one. They tell me this ink is indelible; it'll be a bugger for my daughter to get rid of. But the girl in the mirror disappeared as soon as I began to write, turning her head just once to look over her shoulder and smile as she walked into the distance beyond the back of the fitted wardrobes.

A Straightforward Life

Corrina O'Beirne

Wednesday

There's pornography up the Cinder Path. Found it this morning on my way to pick up *The Daily Herald*. I circled back to the hardware shop on Lullington Avenue, bought a pair of rubber gloves and some bin liners; domestic ones wouldn't be much cop, so I went for industrial strength.

I did my best to clear it; cut my arms to ribbons freeing the pages from the bushes. My footing was all over the shop on account of the sludge (nothing but rain these past nights).

I had a bath when I got home, I felt mucky after handling that filth. Those girls, they've got to be contortionists, bent every which way. One lass was sprawled out with this corn on the cob, smiling away like she was on holiday. I used to enjoy one griddled with a smattering of butter but that's put a stop to it.

It'll be those Sheridan twins. They're the 'top-shelf'

type, borderline feral. The taller one—Billy—well, the sooner he sees a head doctor, the better. Death in his eyes.

I reported it to PC Tomkins, but I've come to expect apathy from that man. How would he like people's bits and pieces grinning at him as he goes about his business? Mother and I class ourselves as Doreton, but (technically) we're Brampton Estate. I've measured it on a map, if we lived 0.6 miles west, we'd be DN3. Tomkins would have a change of attitude then. Granted, the council tax would be higher but I'm a great believer in you get what you pay for.

I shouldn't let him upset me, but it tipped me over the edge this time. Jude came over, bless her socks. I was in a bit of a tizz by the time she arrived. PC Teflon she calls him, which never fails to cheer me. Jude's good with people, she used to be quite a big wig at Allied Carpets. She made me a cup of Horlicks and we shared a piece of toast.

Thursday

Called in on Mother; she's keeping the nurses on their toes! She's paid her stamp, she deserves some attention. We did the crossword together…us Liddles enjoy a little cerebral rejuvenation…we cut through a cryptic like a hot knife through Lurpak. We've been invited to join Mensa more than once, but the test measures a person's cognitive ability compared to the population at large—given the state of this country, what kind of yardstick is that?

Jude popped in with an early Christmas present: a set of these walkie-talkie contraptions! She said it'll cut down on our telephone bills. Oh, we did have a laugh trying them out. She went into the bathroom, I nipped out to the shed.

'Testing, testing. Can you hear me?'

'Crystal clear, Jude!'

So, I, Bernie Liddle, am cordless!

Friday

I took Pepper to the park to do her business and there she was, up to no good by the swings: Kerry Sheridan. Fourteen going on twenty-five, belly like a beanbag. Changes the colour of her hair more often than I change my socks. She wants to get some shampoo on her head, never mind dye.

'Hello, Mr Liddle.' Bold as brass. She has this filthy habit of using the greasy strands of her fringe as dental floss. Always loitering around the precinct—smoking—grin of triumph permanently splashed across her face. Only a matter of time before she's in prison or pregnant, or both.

They've been living on the estate since they were toddlers, so how they can still have that Irish accent is beyond me. Their 'Mammy' as they call her, is built like Geoff Capes, more tattoos than teeth. Forever gallivanting about town when she should be focussed on her kids and the state of her net-curtains.

Saturday

New neighbour. Up from the Isle of Dogs, apparently. Her kiddie was caught up in some gang. Out of all the places in the British Isles, they're plonked next to me. Says she's a part-time psychic, she's done a course.

Oh, I know her type: fast turnover of men, Provident at the door. She'll be on at me with a sob story, wanting money. Knowing people causes nothing but trouble. Us Liddles have a strict policy: leave other people's scar tissue well alone. Not that we are entirely without social inclinations – years back you had good families living here. We all had the same growing up: nothing. But people were kind, proud. The mob that live here now? Sweep them up and dump them somewhere else, preferably the northernmost point of Scotland.

Sunday

The Cinder Path is a state again: Betterware catalogues, a dismantled shower. My bins are spilling over. If I put out more than my allowance, they won't take them. Tony would help me out if he still worked the bins, but he retired last year. Moved to Swansea.

Is it too much to ask to enjoy my haddock loin in peace? The whole tribe on the pavement, dancing around a mobile phone. Screaming the words to some god-awful song in each other's faces, their caterwauling amplified by a hand-mic. Kerry wriggling about like she's got worms, Billy pointing excitedly at absolutely nothing, the shorter one going around in circles with what looks to be a dislocated hip.

8.30p.m. 'Mammy' has joined them, using a soup ladle as a microphone. Laughing. They're always laughing that lot. I'd hate to be there when the laughter stops.

10.15p.m. There's mildew in the shower. This place is going to hell in a handcart. <u>Note to self:</u> buy Cif. <u>Additional note to self:</u> there's no excuse for tardiness when there's nothing else to do.

Monday

I found a nice wild lavender bath set for Jude's Christmas box. The girl at the till gave me an unsolicited look, coupled with a childish comment about a 'lady friend.' Debenhams clearly don't provide adequate training on what constitutes appropriate rapport. I've never looked at Jude that way; I've never looked at anyone that way.

Repeat of *University Challenge*. Mother could wipe the floor with those spotty oiks (such daft names they have: Gideon Figgy-Taxhaven etc). Mother could have walked straight into Oxford or Cambridge but us Liddles think Higher Education is (medical and veterinarian training an exception) self-indulgent hooey.

Mother wouldn't let my mind rot from a mediocre education system. She went toe-to-toe with the local authority until they let her home-school me. I was reciting the chronology of Prime Ministers from Lord Fredrick North through to Attlee by the time I was six.

Tuesday

They've moved Mother to a hospice and the change of scenery has done her good. Before I made it to her bedside to give her a peck, she wheeled out her favourite festive joke:

What did the big angel say to the little angel on Christmas Eve?

Halo there!

Grace Liddle, five foot one, pleated grey skin, hair like spun sugar – still as bright as a knife.

Wednesday

The M&S slippers were a triumph! It really is worth paying a premium for the sheepskin trim – and with the hardwearing sole they'll still be going in five years.

Oh, I am giddy. Mother's been like a frog in a sock all day!

Merry Christmas, diary. Here's to good health and absent friends.

Thursday

Today we had our usual Boxing Day tradition, *Casablanca* paired with a Terry's Chocolate Orange (Mother had the middle wodge, as always!).

I promised her that 2020 would be our year. I don't know how we'd make it to Doreton but make it we would! We'd get one of those semis in a neat cul de sac with the square of green lawn, the air like silk. Somewhere like Lobelia Mews. The gardens on that road are so well-designed with flowers, like walking through a slow-motion fireworks display.

I don't remember drifting off. I woke to find Mother sat bolt upright, her eyes wide open like a newborn, a paper crown balanced on the top of her thin curls. She was lip-syncing Bogart's lines in the final scene.

She wrapped her hand around mine; her skin like tracing paper. Clear plastic tubes disappearing into her, every which way. She began to hum, then sing, her eyes still on the end credits before turning to me, imploring me to join in.

'Sing, Bernie!'

I couldn't…I couldn't fetch up the words. What sort of son sits there like a mute buffoon?

I'm committing to paper that I always preferred Dooley Wilson's version. Not that awful womanizer, Sinatra.

Friday

Saturday

Sunday

Sliced my hand making a sandwich. In a way, the blood was a relief. I watched it run down my wrist … like it was late for something …

There's milk in the fridge so I must've been to the shops, but I don't recall …

My mother is dead.

I haven't been able to say it out loud. I'm writing it down to see what it looks like. The words look foreign, like Sanskrit.

1a.m. Sleep feels far away …

a

pinprick on the horizon. Something horrible

about the middle of the night

you can really hear yourself. The slow, spiteful churning of your organs.

Monday

I woke to find myself at the bottom of the stairs, bruised like a peach. I made an emergency appointment at Brampton surgery. The receptionist was too engrossed in her magazine article (10 NEW WAYS TO WEAR ORANGE) to engage in a little customer care. Yet more evidence of the lamentable decline in common decency. She fobbed me off; said Dr Boyce is on a three-month sabbatical. So, I had to put up with this locum. O'Shea, he called himself.

'You look pale, can I get you a glass of water?' he said.

I informed him that dehydration wasn't the issue. I also got on the front foot and reassured him that us Liddles pride ourselves on being of minimal fuss to the NHS.

'I need some sleeping pills,' I said.

'What makes you think you need sleeping pills?'

'Because I can't sleep.' I laid my words down like playing cards.

'Why don't we talk about what's really bothering you? Pills will only mask the problem.'

'A small pack and I'll be back on an even keel.'

He kept looking at my hands, he knew they were clammy. I saw his pupils dilate with pleasure. They thrive on it, don't they, doctors? They want you on your hands and knees.

Accusing me of being a pill popper! Oh yes, that's why I've muddled through for these past months. I'm not like the mob on the estate. All these mothers claiming the baby blues. Next minute they're up to their eyes on Prozac, Cannabis cigarettes, Heroin. Terrible state. But he wasn't finished, this O'Shea, rattling on about stress, a sudden bereavement.

'Mother was in and out of hospital for seven months,' I said. 'Sudden would have been a blessing. I had to watch her shrink into a bag of bones. Wearing nappies, stewing in her own piddle and muck. I prayed for death. Prayed for it.'

'I can see you're upset.'

'Well, aren't you perceptive? Teach you that at medical school?'

'Grief is like an ocean. Sometimes the water is calm, sometimes it is overwhelming. All one can do, is learn to swim.' He looked at me like he was expecting applause.

'Either way, you're still at sea.'

He whips out this leaflet on grief counselling, pushes it towards me with his bony fingers. Tells me talking therapies are designed to help deal with distressing feelings.

'I know exactly how I feel, that's the point,' I said. 'It's like I've had open heart surgery, but no-one has been good enough to slip me a sedative.'

He looked at his computer screen. Clackety, clack. 'I'd like to refer you,' he said.

'Where, exactly? Butlins?'

When I got to the house, the pain of missing her arrives before me … I can barely get my key in the lock. I'm being eroded, stripped back to the bone, bit by bit.

Tuesday

Library. Some kiddie helped me fire up one of their computers. Three packs of Limovan. Leminat. Or something like that. I couldn't care less as long as they make me sleep.

Wednesday

Her cardigan doesn't smell anymore. I suppose I've used it up. The last of her ghost.

Thursday

The good news is I'm sleeping, the bad news is the pills are playing merry hell with my digestion. I tried some soup but within five minutes I was bringing up blood. What can I do? I need the pills to sleep.

Jude came over because I didn't pick up on the walk-ie-talkie. She found me slumped over the bath, clocked the tablets in my dressing gown pocket and went berserk. Jude's one of these types where her leg would need to be hanging off before she'd consider half a Nurofen.

'These could be horse wormers for all you know.'

I tried to snatch them off her but Jude's quite well-built. She popped every last one from its foil blister, flushed them away. 'You look like death warmed up.'

Never a truer utterance.

Friday

A rotund woman on a disability scooter approached me this morning. Legs thick with diabetes, ratty-looking dog riding pillion in a makeshift basket of cardboard and gaffer-tape.

'You're Bernie Liddle,' she said before coughing extravagantly.

I said nothing, which is usually the safest course of action and instead gave her a look that let her know I was aware of this piece of information. She had this god-awful growth on her neck, not unlike a plum stone.

'I knew your mother. And your father.'

'Yes, like most people I have a mother and a father. Both of which are called Grace.'

I saw her reach for her words. 'My ... condolences.

Loneliness is a bad as cancer. I should know, both have loomed large in my life, hold on to your memories.' And away she wheeled.

I asked Mother once, I must have been about eight. 'The boys were doing their family tree on *Billy Bunter*. Do I have a father?'

'Technically, yes, but he's not anything to write home about.'

So, in the space for Mother, I wrote: Grace Liddle, born 1928. And in the space for Father, I wrote: *technically, yes*.

The only other time I heard a passing reference to *technically, yes*, was when Grandma Liddle referred to him as that 'philandering lump of gristle.'

Monday

That dog has eaten like a Queen. Coley, boiled ham. And she has the audacity to take a treat off that Billy Sheridan. Made up of goodness knows what, pigs' eyes probably. Up on her hind legs, making a fool of me. If Mother were here it would have broken her heart, such duplicity. She never saw eye-to-eye with the Sheridan mother, as well Pepper knows. If she gets a dermatitis flare up, she's on her own. She's in the back room, we're not on speaking terms.

Tuesday

I've led a straightforward life. Nothing especially esoteric, no youthful indiscretions. Well, that's not entirely true, I've encountered the *occasional* fizzle of the grown-up kind. People may say I've missed out and yes, I may never have experienced those fiery flames but on the flip side I've never had to endure the dying embers of love and all that carry on. It's also true that I've never so much as taken a puff on a cigarette. Nothing Gatsbyesque in the life of Bernie Liddle (Mother spared me the ostentatious-ness of a middle name). Unlike many men, I can say, hand on heart that my grey hairs have been honestly earnt.

It's the small things from which I derive the greatest pleasure: a cup of hot tea on a cold morning, the radio is always a source of great solace and a well-constructed sentence can put a bounce in my step all day.

I spent the afternoon following Mother's ghost around from room to room. Touching things: the fruit bowl from Barrow-in-Furness, the framed photo on her bedside table (won at that fair, Mother was great at balloon darts). I thought if I held something she'd held, then I could bring her back for a split second. But the more I tried, the further away she got ... like trying to grab hold of fog ...

I tried Jude a few times on the walkie-talkie, all I got was the sizzle of static. I thought it could be the batteries, so I prised them out and gave them a rub and then it refused to fire up at all.

10.35p.m. Loneliness spreads like moss.

Wednesday

Went to the library. Ten different packs: a medicinal biryani. I paid extra to expedite delivery. They're coming from Latvia.

I've pressed my good suit. I've not bothered with shoes … some unfortunate would only need to prise them off.

Friday

Dear Jude,

If you are reading this then I'm glad for two reasons: it worked, and you found my instructions. I got a bit of a head start and took some of the bulky stuff down to PDSA, everything else is clearly labelled. There's £870 in the blue flask under the sink, a modest legacy but it's yours. Have a nice meal and raise a glass – not to me – to you, you've been a wonderful friend.

Should a woman called Rita (second cousin, red hair) crawl out of the woodwork, please take no notice and don't give her any money, it'll only go on cider and Benylin.

In terms of arrangements, I sorted everything at the same time as Mother, so ask for Iain at the Co-op.

I don't think I've noticed it before, but isn't my penmanship ordinary? Mother's was really quite artistic.

B.

P.s Here's my walkie-talkie (I think it needs new batteries).

Over and out.

Flamingos

Ali McGrane

THE CHILDREN TRAIL after her through the turnstiles. A cloudless sky like an insult, clusters of wooden pointing signs, a peacock dragging finery in the dirt.

Sam ignores his mother's outstretched hand, but moves to her side. Holly swings on her other arm. They choose a path at random.

THE MOULDED SLOPES are clearly meant to mimic packed snow ringing the pool. Kate feels sorry for the lolling penguins, incongruous in the heat. She suppresses the urge to climb in, find sleep among those flightless wings.

Sam reads from the notice. '*Penguin Fun Facts: Penguins swallow seawater while hunting for fish, but a special gland behind their eyes filters out the saltwater from their blood stream and they excrete it through holes in their beaks.* Like tears.'

'Yes.'

'Why do *we* have salty tears?' he says.

Kate thinks of her solemn boy tasting his own tears.

'I'm not sure.'

Something to do with healing, she thinks, as Sam turns back to the words.

'Many birds have hollow bones to help them fly, but penguins have dense bones which makes diving easier.'

Holly spins on one foot, chanting gibberish.

'Hush,' Kate says. 'Sam's speaking.'

Holly crashes into the fence and slides to the ground, a fixed grin on her face. Kate imagines an effortless descent. The wrap of water. Silence.

Sam goes on. *'Penguins undergo a process called catastrophic moulting, when they replace all their feathers in the space of a few weeks.'*

The day Jay left he did everything as usual. Herding the kids, coffee and toast, the morning-rush goodbyes. No clues.

At midday, an impossible text, a sign-off that made no sense: *don't look for me, I'm sorry, be happy.*

Then nothing.

'Mum?'

Sam's face is level with her own.

'Get up, Mum.'

She rises from her crouch, clutches the railing, and musters herself. Penguins queue to flop into the water, toppling like dominoes.

THE SUBTERRANEAN VIEWING station is cool and dark. Through thick distorting glass they watch torpedo bodies dart and weave in an illusion of flight.

BACK UNDER THE sun, Sam finds a sign for pet's corner. Holly bounces at his shoulder. They lead on, united in purpose for once, to a scrubby stretch of grass and dandelions, a scatter of hutches and small pens. Guinea pigs, rabbits, bantams. A pygmy goat. Two lambs. Kate takes a seat on the edge.

'Teeth and claws.' The woman's face is half-hidden under a tatty straw hat. Her hands worry in her lap.

'Sorry?'

'All that fluff and cuteness.'

It's hard to know how to respond. Kate watches her children, Sam on his knees by the rabbit pen, Holly tearing up handfuls of grass for the eager goat. Jay had always refused their pleas for a pet.

'The wild will out.' The woman makes her words punch the air, like a curse. People are looking.

'The wild, yes.' Agreeing to keep the peace. This, Kate understands.

Holly's wail explodes from the river of human and animal noise, and Kate is on her feet, without conscious thought. She homes in on her frantic daughter, on the tiny goat chomping and tugging at her t-shirt. From the look on Holly's face, hysterical laughter is not going to help.

BY THE TIME they join the queue for the boat trip, the sky is leaden. Kate shivers. The cries of the gibbons echo among the trees.

Sam and Holly squeeze into a space at the prow. The smell of fuel is sickening as the engine surges, then settles into a bone-shaking throb. A loudspeaker stutters over the din.

'Welcome to Gibbon Island, home to our small tribe. Gibbons are the most agile of all the apes. Their long arms and hooked hands help them swing through the branches at speeds of up to thirty-five miles an hour, and they can leap up to ten metres from a standing start.'

She's back in the school gym, slippery wall bars, hanging twists of fat jute, air rank with decades of adolescent posturing and shame. She's climbed a rope, hand over hand to the highest point, is resting with her arm hooked over the rigging, looking down on her oblivious classmates as they fall to the chaser's tag. Waiting till she can reveal herself as the last one standing. Jay taught her that trick. At sixteen they were already a couple, skin to skin, sharing all the crazy stuff in each other's heads. How could she not know what he was feeling?

Sam's hand burrows into her clenched fist.

Holly is squeaking about the baby gibbon, cleaved to its mother's chest as she loops from tree to tree. The mother hangs by one arm, directly above them, swinging gently, and there is a remoteness in the animal's gaze that reminds Kate of beggars in the street. As though it has left the spark of itself in some other place. The engine quiets to a low thrum as the boat slows on the turn, and the crackling voice resumes.

'Gibbons can be identified by their song. Their morning calls fill the tropical rainforests with sound. Gibbons mate for life and sing a duet every day to strengthen their bond. Each pair's call is unique.'

The laden boat ploughs back to the jetty, the bow wave unfolding and spreading in its wake.

GIANT SPOTS OF summer rain needle her skin and spatter the hot path. That metallic tang, all their summers twisted in the tell of it, and she flees, dodging wildly. The children give chase. She swerves across the grass and into a picnic shelter, hurls herself onto the rough bench. They fall into her, a litter of limbs, panting half-laughs. She slumps, weak with knowing, with the high walls to be scaled, with the way their blood pulses and their bones inexorably grow.

'Giraffes next,' she says, pushing them off and stretching up, tall as she can.

THE WALKWAY TAKES them out over the paddock, level with the crowns of trees. Three giraffes amble and chew. The word leggy was made for them.

Kate holds down the ripped corner of a faded notice and reads what's left, '*Giraffe Fun Facts: The giraffe is the tallest land animal in the world, standing up to five and a half metres high. Each giraffe has its own pattern of markings, like a fingerprint. No two are the same.*'

Sam studies his fingers. 'So they can't tell just by looking?'

'Tell what?'

'Who belongs to who.'

Kate strokes the soft pads of his fingertips, wordless.

Sam reads on for her. He's a good reader but she wishes he would stop. '*In the wild, males and females often live separately, only coming together to mate. Babies are nearly two metres tall when they're born, and grow two centimetres a day. Their first experience of life is a long drop to the ground, because female giraffes give birth standing up.*'

If she'd thought about having babies at all, it was part of some unimaginable future where she might be ready to do grown-up things. She was five months gone before they even realised she was pregnant, and when she saw the scan there was nothing to do but keep going.

Holly wriggles between them, holding out her spread fingers.

'Look at mine.'

Kate gathers all their hands in her own. She can't make them fit, and they squirm and slide free.

ON THE CAFÉ terrace, flocks of sparrows whirr past her ears like clockwork toys. Holly makes a pyramid of breadcrumbs and the thronging birds swoop.

'Take a picture, Mum,' Holly whispers.

Kate is already framing it in her phone. She snaps again and again, stockpiling for lean times ahead.

AFTER LUNCH SAM wants to see the dragon. Kate explains what a Komodo dragon is, but they're not listening. The stories are written on their faces. She shrugs.

'Go on, then.' She points to the reptile house sign. 'Here be dragons!'

They run ahead, hover, run some more, fear and excitement visibly battling. It's too easy to press their switches, too easy to get it wrong. The potential to do harm. She hurries to catch them before they disappear through the doorway.

Her blood slows and thickens. Exotic lizards flicker across miniature landscapes under fake suns. A python ripples from sleeping coils. Holly stands transfixed before a tank filled with tiny acid-yellow frogs. Grotesque jewels with bulging eyes and throats. The air is a physical barrier,

close and moist and hot. It stops speech. Sam points and
tugs. Here be dragons.

They follow him under an archway. People shuffle at
the rail. A snout rests on a flat rock, its body disguised
behind tropical greenery.

'Where's the dragon?' Holly says.

Kate picks her up. She's almost too big for it now but
she clings. Nestles her head.

'There are different kinds of dragons,' Kate says.

Sam passes one of the big black phones. He holds
another close to his ear. They listen, separately and
together.

*'Komodo Dragons are the world's largest and most dan-
gerous lizard. Like snakes, they use their forked tongues to
sample the air and scent their prey. Komodo dragons lay eggs
in a hole in the ground. Baby dragons climb into a tree as
soon as they hatch, to avoid being eaten by their mother or
other Komodos.'*

Oh, the tired and glorious trance of it. Her lips glued
to velvet cheeks, to milk-fat bellies, the salty taste of
womb-creased soles. Kate lowers Holly to the ground,
squats beside her, their two heads pressed to the device,
the disconnected voice.

*'Komodo dragons are fierce carnivores with sharp claws
and serrated teeth. They eat anything they can catch,
including wild pigs, deer, water buffalo and even humans.
The poisonous bacteria in their saliva means that even if an*

animal escapes, it often dies within twenty-four hours.'

Sam makes a yuck face and grins, his father's grin. Behind him the dragon emerges and tongues the air. His scales are gold and grey.

'Will he grow wings?' says Holly.

'He might,' Kate hears herself answer. And almost believes it.

THE CHILDREN SCURRY to Kate's loping strides, and it's as though the earth has mislaid its gravity, or their bones have been hollowed out. She takes them over the hill to the lake, a gleaming body of water surrounded by reed beds. Easy afternoon sun. Flamingos.

Armed with ice creams, they find a spot on the bank with a view of the birds. The balletic harmony of back-bent legs and sinuous necks. A wonderland of scooping bills. There may not be a better moment. She waits while they finish their cones. Listens to a distant gibbon's song.

'I know you miss your dad,' she says, looking from one to the other, not wanting to miss a thing. 'I miss him too. I'm sorry I can't tell you why he left, or where he's gone.' She stops, her throat raked raw by the words.

Holly shuffles closer. Sam hunches.

'But I can tell you this. He loves you both, and that will never change, wherever he is, whatever he does. You're part of him and he …'

She reaches out to touch her son. He turns and opens. It's too much.

'… he's a beautiful part of you.'

'Don't cry, Mum,' Holly says, tears spilling.

Kate pulls them to her, the armour of their bodies like a second skin.

DOWN BY THE reeds, the colony of flamingos performs its slow dance, breaking the placid surface of the water into a thousand eddies. Kate scans the notice for fun facts to read aloud. She picks two.

'Although they're most often seen just wading, flamingos are strong swimmers and powerful fliers.

The word flamingo means fire.'

Centuries, in Burnt Sienna

Nastasya Parker

MY SISTER DEVOURED all history, beginning in the summer vacation when she was six. The century soon ending was Tabitha's starter. She told me barbed wire cut her lip and toxic fumes tainted everything. Some of it was outer-space-cold, some burning-rainforest-hot.

I was five at the time and unimpressed, particularly when she commandeered my Lego train bricks to show me what a concentration camp looked like. 'Only it wouldn't be these bright colours,' she said.

Then Tabitha ate the preceding century. The first tastes were all right: ocean salt and prairie grass. But it got worse. She choked on hot metal chains. Cotton stopped her tongue for a while, and she insisted if I didn't see steam or coal smoke coming out her ears, I wasn't looking hard enough.

'Why would I look for that?' I went back to playing Barbies.

Tabitha was rubbish at Barbies. As soon as I got Cindy into a hot pink strapless gown and tiny gold heels, Tabitha snatched her away. 'Those clothes are pointless.'

'Nuh-uh, she's going to a ball.' I grabbed Cindy by her skirt, and the dress came off in my hand as Tabitha peeled it back.

'That's boring. She's going West on the Oregon trail with the others, and at least three of them will die. She won't even have toilet paper.'

In September she went back another century, to make sure her new teachers recognised how smart she was. This wedge of history had nice spices and silken textures apparently, but ended with gunpowder singeing her throat and blades scalding her tongue.

I didn't look up from my colouring. Dad had brought home a whole printer paper ream, perforations on the sides, and I tried our jumbo crayon set on it. Some colours got only patches, some I gave great swathes.

'April,' Tabitha said, 'you're not even making anything.'

'I'm making colours.' I scowled at her and ripped off a side strip, slowly and menacingly.

Tabitha ate two more centuries that school year. 'It's partly because there's less available to read about them,' she explained, 'so I might as well do two.' She had splinters of shipmast in her cheek and warm winds of exploration dispelled revolutionary smoke, until she uncovered blazes of execution. She grimaced at the sourness of disease, cruelty delivered in iambic pentameter. She wiped thick oil paint and plaster dust from her lips. 'At least people did a few good things, too.'

'Whoop-de-doo.' I spun my homework book, unopened, on the kitchen table.

'Don't you want to improve your reading?' my parents and teacher had said at the latest meeting. 'You could be as talented as your sister if you tried.'

While Mom and Dad positioned Tabitha's report card on the fridge and she opened the encyclopedia to learn more about Japan's Onin War, I flipped to the back of the picture book assigned to me and drew clown shoes on the prince's feet.

In third grade, Tabitha gulped down at least a millennium, gritty with dirt and wriggling with jungle flavours from civilisations flourishing elsewhere, all awash on streams of Communion wine. 'The further back I go, people find weirder ways to hurt each other,' she told me, slumped on the stone wall, fingering a volume about human sacrifices in old Central America.

I jumped with both feet into the pile of leaves Mom had raked in the back yard. 'So why read that stuff?'

'Everyone says people used to be good, and not obsessed with silly things like TV and shopping. I just haven't found when they were actually *better*.'

I rolled onto my back and made an angel, swishing my arms and legs, squinting through falling leaf matter at the cloudy November sky. 'That's what you get for listening to grown-ups.' I let the leaf pile collapse over me. So many shades of brown on the ground, and greys in the sky. I loved them all, as much as the last yellows and reds grasping the trees, and the blue failing to elbow through the storm.

Yet when I drew a November picture for school, using every hue of umber and sienna and chestnut and chocolate and charcoal I could find, my teacher said it wasn't bright enough for the classroom display. 'You couldn't have coloured a sunny day?'

I blew a raspberry at her and walked out, taking myself to the principal's office without being told. While he lectured me, I watched my frown reflected in his black shoes, shiny to the point of colourlessness. I drew sunny days sometimes. I just didn't want to overlook grey.

Tabitha ate as far back as she could. She finished elementary school with Neolithic boulders in her stomach and saber-toothed tiger gristle in her teeth. By the time I joined her at the Junior High, she'd regurgitated everything she read, and the things once stuck in her throat muffled the teachers ears from hearing me. I slouched at my desk and doodled, ignoring assignments.

Ivy League colleges courted Tabitha before she was sixteen. History had only been the first course; she was invited to an event in Washington, D.C. and began devouring politics. 'When we call something unprecedented,' she said, 'all this means is our contemporary human brains can't grasp the magnitude of events, many of them tragic, which have come before.'

'Right.' I slid a pastel over my paper. I'd graduated from crayons but remembered all the names, reciting them in my head when I was bored at school or couldn't sleep. When sleep overtook me, sometimes the colours married and birthed beautiful new hues I couldn't recall in the morning.

'Let's talk about your goals,' said the high school guidance counsellor.

I kicked my metal chair legs and shrugged at the dingy floor tiles. 'I'm going to refurbish an abandoned shed and call it Burnt Sienna. I'll live there and do art with a puppy named Periwinkle and a pygmy goat named Ochre.'

Meanwhile, Tabitha was a Model Congress star headed to Yale on a full scholarship. 'It's not enough to read everything,' she informed me as if I were at risk of doing that. 'I need the right letters after my name, so people will listen, and then maybe I can make everyone stop blindly swallowing reckless indulgences, as humanity has done since crawling out of the oceans.'

I paused while painting in my left eyebrow. 'Wasn't crawling out of the ocean an indulgence in the first place?'

'Of course. I'm not against progress, April; there's not much in those earlier times I wish to return to. But history teaches that we're not infallible, and a modicum of awareness is …'

I smothered her justifications in a crackling cloud of hairspray. Tabitha choked. 'You look like a sarcophagus,' she snapped on her way out of my room.

Whatever I looked like, boys enjoyed it. I experimented with at least a third of the boys in my class, allowing them space on the long printer paper roll of my life. A few bright ones I scribbled with briefly, but mostly they were greys and browns: C students driving beat-up Fords or Pontiacs and still imitating Kurt Cobain several years after his death.

'Who are you looking for?' Tabitha asked. 'It's not good for you, all this … *playing around.*' After her first couple years of college, missing my high school graduation while interning at the Capitol, she visited home with a studious girlfriend.

The girlfriend was listening politely while Dad showed off the refinished kitchen cupboards. Her hands, clasped behind her back, were chapped and fidgeting.

I straightened my Craftworld tabard, on my way to eight hours of telling people which aisle had glitter pens, and arguing with expectant mothers about an extra half-inch of Winnie-the-Pooh fabric. 'It's not bad for me, either. You've found someone just as scared of the world as you are—congratulations. I don't need to because it doesn't scare me, since I wasn't stupid enough to learn all about it.'

But as Tabitha began her third year at college, the world got my attention. The store was quiet that Tuesday morning, just a few moms enjoying their regained time now kids were back in school. The manager rushed us through checking out their orders and locked the doors. On the computer in the back office we watched the first tower fall. The pixellated screen showed ominous greys roiling over the perfect blue sky, just a four-hour drive away.

My parents were frantic. Tabitha had been visiting Washington, scheduled to fly home that afternoon. She was so extraordinary, you'd think the terrorists organised the whole thing to take Tabitha down. She was fine, of course.

'Did you know this would happen?' I asked when she called. Behind me, CNN repeated footage of bodies leaping past blue, disappearing into grey. 'You must have read about precedents.'

'Enough to know that what's next is bound to hurt even more people.'

She took a train home. We sat beside each other at the kitchen table with the newspaper in front of us. She guzzled the mini-biographies of the dead while I drank the faces in their many shades. 'I don't blame you for being mad at me.' Tabitha clutched her stomach. I could taste what she did; I knew how bitterly the ash lingered, how warped rebar scraped her insides.

'I'm not.' I turned the page. More faces. 'It wasn't your job to stop this, Tabitha. You're not that important.'

I felt her relax next to me, her grip on her abdomen slacking. She stared ahead at the kitchen window, for once not swallowing every printed word placed before her. 'Thanks. Sometimes I'm sad you don't do art anymore.'

'I do art. Yesterday I arranged the fabric paint shelf so all the tubes are in colour order.'

It wasn't enough now, though. I felt what Tabitha must have, most of her life: full of something I must somehow bleed out. I stayed up late, sketching those faces from the newspaper. Tabitha finished college, alternating between Yale and Washington. I enrolled in an LNA course to help at hospitals when the next attack came. It might be biological, nuclear … I tried not to doodle too much in my anatomy textbooks.

'There won't be more attacks,' Tabitha informed me as the Taliban fled to their caves. 'Great empires always extinguish external threats after an incursion. We'll crumble eventually, but from within.' She sighed over the phone from Washington, where she tried to schedule meetings and work her way up to talk to more important people. 'The deaths don't seem to mean much to them.'

'They probably only read about things, they never ate it.' My diagram of the circulatory system swam before my tired eyes. The body was portrayed in such garish colours.

Again Tabitha thanked me, as if I'd said something profound. She reformed her whole Master's thesis. Instead of some vast inedible mess charting humanity through history, it became a pedagogical work on making history's lessons palatable for the War on Terror.

She graduated with top honours in the winter. Mom made a big cave cake to celebrate, complete with fondant Neanderthals and a strawberry bloom fire. I don't think my parents read the thesis. I never got my bedpan-handling fingers on it either, my eyes done at the end of long shifts seeking veins and checking bedsores. We weren't her target audience, anyway. Tabitha brought her work to the capital, delivering presentations in identical hotel conference rooms, treading cautiously around fleur-de-lys carpet patterns and politicians' convictions. Wood panel polish fumes, waxy fruit, and civil servant cologne sustained her.

Meanwhile the rest of the nation subsisted on a diet of beefed-up intelligence. The War on Terror expanded. At first I gobbled it up, as our parents did. I was ready for anything that would inject more meaning into my work, and apparently several former classmates were too. Boys I sometimes still met in Pontiac backseats hoiked up their trousers, cut their hair, and enlisted.

Tabitha pried the notions from our jaws. 'The confidence you see on TV—It's different here,' she noted. 'They're nervous.' Beneath the shock and awe spices and

the Mission Accomplished frosting, she detected re-
sistance, from the flinty flavours of the Celts defying the
Romans, to the poison vapours of the Iraq-Iran war.

Twenty years after eating all of history, Tabitha
changed her diet. She gorged on the Mesopotamian
Arabic language in just one month, peppered by palatals
and pharyngeals. She unhinged her jaws to gulp construction manuals, steadily imbibed security contracts, and
spewed out funding pages. Then she left, to build her
girls' school near Mosul, including a teaching institute,
sowing a scholarly crop on The Fertile Crescent.

I visited annually to give courses on feminine health.
Tabitha also had me lead art therapy groups. I supplied
Crayola sets. Raw sienna was a favourite, and sea green.
Tabitha and I watched sunrises over Ninevah on the
opposite bank of the Tigris before each busy workday,
days interrupted by power outages, updates on insurgency
movements, or 'friendly' fire nearby.

Tabitha was among the first to taste the changes in
the musky air. She raised extra money for a compound,
starting with huts for Yazidis and others fleeing from the
West. Insurgency leavened and baked into a caliphate.
Tabitha made an emergency trip to Washington but
found no answers to sink her teeth into.

On my last visit, I lay on my back by the Tigris. I
waved my arms till they tingled, and I could barely indent
the packed sand on its banks. It was grey-brown, the

colour of falling asleep, and the sky a dim yellow-pink, obscuring any hints of which way the weather would turn. I remembered my childhood leaf angel drawing. I might occasionally have hoped, but never dreamed, that Tabitha and her home would one day be as unappreciated as I felt then.

'Assyrians marched along here,' Tabitha said, 'And Babylonians, Persians, Turks and Mongols. This beach is ground down from seashells, you know.'

'Maybe the same ones our ancestors wore when they crawled out of the sea?'

She laughed. 'They wouldn't have had shells, silly.'

Before I left I drew a shell for her on a sheet of construction paper, earthy umber on the outside but pastel pearlescent within. It was no match for the shells Daesh fired. Some of Tabitha's students and their families escaped. She'd found homes overseas for a few of the already-orphaned, her old DC contacts finally proving useful at circumventing red tape. The so-called caliphate devoured priceless Assyrian artefacts, the remaining Christians and hundreds more, and my sister. It vomited more atrocities onto our screens, until my parents and I were glad Tabitha didn't survive the first missiles. What came after looked worse.

My grief was gritty and frantic, metallic and hot. The turmoil of my new daily life ground it down to a powder through which I moved in slow-motion. But I keep moving.

I got a mobile home and I'm taking a break from my hospital job. I make some money doing pet portraits, late at night, no bright colours necessary. Plus, Tabitha left me what she could. My parents found me a puppy I named Periwinkle, and in my trailer's kitchen, I have a jar for loose change. I'm saving for a pygmy goat. The girls will love it.

'Aunt April, Periwinkle tried to eat the cornflower crayon.' Eskere brings me the crayon, its paper scraped away by canine fangs. Cornflower is her colour; we use it on the family calendar to mark Girl Scout meetings, drum lessons, and Yazidi holidays.

'Crayons are good,' Rahima says. 'They make my teeth rub smooth together.' Her Sunni holidays and dance classes are cerise on the calendar.

Our calendar is also filled with therapy appointments and check-ups. The girls have gulped down English and have a healthy appetite for TV, but they still bear the teethmarks of loss and trauma. They may never call me Mom, but when they say 'Aunt April,' it sounds like spring green.

'Don't eat crayons,' Eskere chides.

'I just tasted it …' They exchange Arabic insults not included in the guides Tabitha sent me, arguing as only sisters can. Black ponytails swish and hand-painted macaroni necklaces rattle.

I step away from stacking lunchtime dishes. The sink is currently in use as a deep sea diving site for Barbies to investigate Lego Atlantis. We chose dolls in shades from tumbleweed to Van Dyke brown. They're wearing evening gowns, plus hard hats to protect against sharks. We pass the afternoon cradling Periwinkle, watching for blue flowers sprouting from his tummy, because when you swallow something, you never know how it can change you.

Phylum

Rhys Timpson

MOIRA HATED INSECTS. It was the one thing she shared with her stepfather. Gareth would shiver at the sight of a spider and reach for the cordless vacuum. Her mother was different; she would cradle spiders in her hands and carry them outside, their legs poking between her fingers.

Moira knew spiders weren't really insects, of course; that was playground wisdom. But it didn't matter. Insects or arachnids, the scuttling, crawling creatures of the earth were things to be eradicated, not to live alongside.

This was why the sight of the earwig on the kitchen table was so disgusting. That it seemed to have dropped from her mother's nose made it only more so.

'It's all right,' Moira's mother said. She put her toast down and nudged the animal onto its front with a fingertip, then let it crawl up into her palm. '*Forficula auricularia*,' she said. 'A female. You can tell by its pincers. Male ones are curved.'

'It came out of your *nose*,' Moira said, aghast.

Her mother smiled and shrugged as if it were nothing, then let the insect climb a little further before she placed a finger on her wrist and transferred it to her other hand. Its shell was brown and waxy. She took it to the back door and laid it on a paving stone just beyond the step.

Moira's father had been an entomologist. She'd heard the word from a young age but had only fairly recently mastered its twists and turns. Her mother had adopted her father's vocation as if it were her own, as a way of keeping part of him alive. Moira had only faint memories of him, old wounds she would sometimes probe to see if they still hurt: the squeak of shoes on hospital floors, the beep of machinery, the stench of bleach, a waving hand. They had kept him behind glass in a special room, like an animal at a zoo. He'd come back from the Amazon a week before and they said whatever he had might be infectious. There were some pictures of him in the house, hidden in drawers and at the bottom of her mother's wardrobe. He had been tall and athletic, with curly black hair that was one of the few things he had left to his daughter. Moira knew he was dead, but sometimes she pictured him in a jungle somewhere, machete in hand, sweat on his brow, searching for a way back to them.

It was the summer holidays, and Moira was spending the morning with her mother in the town library. Her mother was the head librarian, the little stone building her sovereign domain. Moira sat by the misted-up windows and looked out at the pedestrians in the street below. There were some old people at the back of the building flicking through large-print books, a homeless man who came in for warmth and to read thrillers, and some mothers with pushchairs who would come and go as their toddlers demanded, the children's cries the only sound that broke the reverential silence. Moira was bored, but it was an enjoyable boredom. She did a circuit of the building and then stopped by the front desk to talk to her mother, finding her deeply engrossed in an old hardback book with a sun-bleached cover.

'One of your father's favourites,' her mother said, putting it down on the counter. 'I think it may have been the last thing he read.' She dabbed her eyes with a tissue and looked away.

At midday, Gareth finished his minicab shift and came to pick Moira up, creeping across the tiled floor and whispering as if he were interrupting a church service. As she waved goodbye, Moira saw a black fly crawling along the lapel of her mother's blouse, its fat body millimetres away from the pale skin of her neck.

Gareth took Moira swimming and then they went home, where she sat on the sofa playing with her wet hair and made fitful progress calculating probabilities for her maths homework. She was back to daydreaming about the distant rainforest when Gareth shouted and jumped to his feet.

'Jesus Christ,' he said. A large black beetle was sitting on the empty sofa cushion beside him, its antennae twitching as it responded to some unknowable stimulus. Moira wanted to kill it, but something about the disparity between its tiny body and her own made her stop. Gareth fetched a glass from the kitchen, and soon the unfortunate creature was imprisoned under an invisible dome. Her stepfather retreated to the armchair, sipping his tea and glowering at the intruder. Moira turned back to her homework, but she couldn't concentrate. She was thinking about the beetle and its dwindling supply of air.

When her mother came home, Moira rushed to the hallway to tell her about the captive insect but found herself waved away. Her mother was coughing and holding a clump of tissues over her mouth, her forehead shiny with sweat. 'I feel awful,' she said. 'I'm going for a lie-down.' Moira stood on the threshold of the living room and looked between the staircase and the sofa. The beetle hadn't moved in a long time.

Her mother didn't get up for the rest of the evening. Gareth cooked a shepherd's pie, which they ate in relative silence. Just before bedtime, Moira slipped an old birthday card under the glass holding the beetle and released it onto the back step, holding it as far away from her body as her arms would allow.

The next morning, Moira came downstairs to find Gareth in the kitchen, pouring tea with one hand and taking a bite of toast with the other. 'Your mum's not feeling well still,' he said. 'Fancy an egg?'

After she had eaten, Moira took her mother a cup of tea. She found her asleep, the duvet wrapped tight around her. The curtains were closed, the room subterranean in the russet light. She set the mug down on the bedside table, pushing her father's old book towards the lamp. Her mother's face was pale and shiny.

Above the bed, two large flies darted around each other in a helical pattern, always on the verge of collision. She picked up the book and shooed them away, but they reconvened a little more towards the ceiling where she couldn't reach them.

The book was called *The Hidden Phylum*, a title impenetrable enough to pique Moira's curiosity. She took it back to her room and sat on her bed, where it fell open to a double-page spread of pictures of beetles. The drawings made the insects look beautiful, their shells bright and colourful, their hooked black legs not frightening but elegant. She turned the pages, whispering the Latin names of the arthropods like an incantation: *Panagaeus bipustulatus, Pholcus phalangioides, Sarcophaga bercaea*.

The next morning, she found Gareth on the sofa, his black fleece dressing gown draped over him as a makeshift blanket, the cordless vacuum by his side. 'Morning, love,' he said. 'Thought I'd give your mum a bit of space. She's a bit poorly still. You want some toast? Or an egg? Toast and an egg?'

He cooked her breakfast and let her watch some television, but she couldn't settle on anything. One slice of her toast was black around the edges and the other was little more than warm bread, its pitted surface still spongiform and soft. In the hallway, she heard Gareth going up and down the stairs. Peering around the door, she saw him carrying bedsheets tied in a bundle. 'Just getting some washing on,' he said. There was an acrid smell in the air, like disinfectant and bad perfume. Her stepfather opened the back door and carried the sheets outside and round to the alley, to the place they kept the bins.

Moira was four steps up to the landing when Gareth came back in. 'Your mum's sleeping, love,' he said. 'Best not to wake her.' He washed his hands under the sink, keeping them there even as the warm water turned hot and started to send up steam.

Moira retreated to the living room and thought about her mother, about what she would do if anyone tried to take her away. The thought was impossible to hold; it made her feel as if she were about to break apart. 'Gareth,' she said. 'Can I see Mum?'

'She's resting,' he said. He was holding a dust mask and a pair of rubber gloves. 'Just some odd jobs need doing.'

She waited until she heard him reach the landing,

then crept to the bottom of the stairs. She heard some-thing being sprayed and the sound of the vacuum cleaner, and then the door opened again. Gareth was wearing the dust mask and gloves and carrying a black canister. She darted back to the living room just before he reached the stairs.

'I need to make a phone call – work thing,' Gareth said, looking in on her. He walked hunched over, as if he'd been punched, and he was shaking. He closed the door, pulling it all the way shut and turning the handle, then dialled three digits that caused a sudden nausea to well up inside Moira. She waited until she heard him walk down the hall and opened the door a little. He was stepping into the back garden. When he looked away, she took her chance.

The first thing she noticed as she climbed the steps was the strata of smells: the fake pine of the air freshener and the aggressive pungency of detergent, and beneath them both something deeper – the scent of wet leaves and damp earth, the stench of decay. As she climbed into the darkness of the landing, she heard a series of light taps, like something knocking on the floor. Her mother's door was closed. She put her fingers on the handle and turned.

The bed had been stripped; her mother lay on a bare mattress in her pyjamas, the duvet piled in the corner. The window was open, a light breeze making the curtains look as if they were breathing. Her mother was tied to the bedposts with four pairs of black tights, the knocking sound caused by the headboard tapping the wall as she pulled at her binds. Moira started forward, heart battering her ribs, but then stopped.

Flies hung over her mother in a black cloud, a trail of ants circumnavigated her body like supplicants on a prayer path. Black dots crawled on the exposed skin where her top had risen over her waist. Moira started to back out, but then her mother lifted her head and looked at her, her pupils two swollen black discs. 'Moira,' she whispered. Her voice was a low rattle, as if the air were being drawn through a small channel full of obstacles. Moira took a step closer, but that was all she could do. Something long and thin moved beneath the fabric of the left leg of her mother's pyjamas. 'Don't be afraid,' she said. Moira inched forward again but then stopped, looked back over her shoulder, and thought about Gareth. 'They're coming to take me,' her mother said.

She took the last few steps and reached out for the first of the binds. There was a spider crawling up the bedpost, probing the wood with its spindly legs. She closed her eyes and slipped the knot apart. Then she moved to the next one.

There were beetles on her mother's ankle, their coal-black shells in stark contrast to the pale skin. Moira untied the tights and then stifled a scream as an earwig dropped onto the carpet. Looking down, she saw a writhing mass of things beneath the bed, crawling and clambering over each other in the shadows. She felt light-headed, looked back towards the door, but then proceeded to the last two bindings.

Her mother reached out a hand, but as Moira took it, she felt something hard and chitinous crawl into the gap between her fingers. She pulled away, whimpering, and the black thing fell to the floor. 'Please,' her mother said. And then she heard sirens in the distance, and she clasped her mother's fingers in her own.

They made it to the landing, and then the stairs. With each step, Moira wanted to pull away, to shake off the things crawling onto her, transferring their tiny forms from her mother's body onto hers. She wanted to scream and cry, but her mother needed help to walk. She didn't look and tried not to listen to the sounds of small, heavy things falling onto the carpet.

The front door was open; Gareth was standing in the porch and shouting to the paramedics as they parked the ambulance. He turned as Moira and her mother reached the hallway. She could see the horror on his face, but she dared not look at her mother herself. Something pushing its way into her hair. She pulled her mother towards the kitchen. 'Stop,' Gareth said, but it was a plea, not a command. He made no move towards them.

Her mother seemed to be gaining strength, so that by the time they reached the back door she was the one doing the pulling. They stepped out into the garden just as the paramedics stepped into the house. Moira could hear the crackling chatter on their radios.

'What do we do?' she said. Her mother took Moira's face in her hands, the skin of her palms cold yet pulsing with life. Moira closed her eyes. And her mother held her there, a thousand tiny forms pushing against her epidermal veil. 'Goodbye,' she whispered. And then she ran.

Moira opened her eyes to see her mother bounding across the patio and the lawn, then slipping into the woods beyond the back gate. She ran after her, shouting for her to stop. As she caught sight of her mother for the last time, she saw the stream of life falling from her beginning to narrow, her mother's feet and calves disintegrating as she collapsed into the carpet of leaves and water-logged ground. Moira slipped and fell into the miasma. When she looked up, her mother was gone. She called out, sinking her hands into the forest floor – that thriving sea of decay. Worms wrapped around her fingers and beetles pushed into her palms, wet leaves sank into the loam. She had the feeling of everything moving into everything else and, in that, there was something like an answer.

Spinach, Celery, Carrot, Beetroot, Ginger, Apple

Henry Heffer

THERE'S A COOKBOOK catering to every diet imaginable, and each is its own small religion. In the top floor flat we can barely afford, our cookbook has its own shelf in the kitchen. Multicoloured post-it notes poke out of its pages like a tasselled carnival outfit. 'It's a diet. It begins with a Cleansing. But don't worry, it's all natural.' No longer will she rely on topical steroids, she says she must break free from their power. So too, her profiles. Stuffed with avocado ice-creams, beetroot burgers, gluten-free, dairy-free, flavour-free false idols. All just a distraction from the one true path those that suffer must take. But it begins with a Cleansing. It's the first chapter of the book. It is the Genesis.

One juice, three times a day. Breakfast, lunch and dinner. For seven days. Ingredients: spinach, celery, carrot, beetroot, ginger, apple. Just enough to fill a small wine glass. Seven days. Only seven days.

***

Monday

SHE'S READ THE book cover to cover, twice. I catch her in empty moments passing the pages between her fingers, like a nun praying the Rosary. She sits up at night looking longingly at the photographs of shiny, pastel-coloured food, but there are also some of the author – these are the ones she spends most her time with. The author's a woman with perfect white skin, bouncy blonde hair, dressed all in white. Her kitchen is just as white and clean. And she smiles in each photograph, as if everything – absolutely everything – is going to be alright.

I watch her read and reread the introduction, glee upon her face. It's been fifteen years, the steroid creams was all she knew. But now, this will be the beginning of a whole new beginning.

After work she goes to the supermarket. Our kitchen's suddenly overflowing with fruit and veg. Turmeric capsules, Dead Sea bath salts, shea butter, milk thistle and charcoal toothpaste. Pride of place is the new juicer. It removes the pulp you see, producing a nectar the same colour and consistency of the primordial ponds where life began. She strips off her clothes and spends an hour and a half putting all of it in its rightful place. Then she prepares the first day's worth, full of visions of herself as a smooth carapace of brown flesh, like the sleek hull of some high-tech alien spaceship. Finally, eyelids moving rapaciously at the content of her dreams, she falls asleep in my arms.

And so it begins.

Tuesday

COME SIX O'CLOCK, after work, she's tired but excited. Proudly she slurps down her first dinner juice, and eyeballs my tuna steaks. 'Did you know she went through all that pain and suffering so that we now know about the Cleansing?'

'Yes, my love.'

Wednesday

SHE'S OUT OF the house before I'm up. So I send her a text at midday, telling her I'm proud of her. In my hour alone after work I clean the entire flat, but when she returns home she's grumpy and barely acknowledges it. She frowns down half her dinner juice, then lets the other half sit for an hour before polishing it off in one grimace.

In bed I try and talk with her about Yemen. Big mistake.

Thursday

THE STEROIDS ARE no longer holding back the truth about her skin. The redness that had consumed her as an adolescent, has returned. It runs up both her triceps, like hipster sleeve tattoos. Then cracks like thin ice, into crinkled shards. She tells me it hurts. I don't doubt it.

That night, as we watch a film sat on the sofa, she unexpectedly bursts into tears. Holding her (with the utmost care) I feel the hot dots of healing skin against my torso, it's like I'm lying on my belly across sun-bleached pebbles at the beach. I tell her she's very brave. Which she is.

Friday

SHE COMES HOME swinging. Cleans the fridge out, then sits in a lukewarm bath for two hours, the salt content of which should resemble the Dead Sea. Her skin has yielded yet more ground to the redness. I watch from the doorway as her body breaches the water – a collection of ruby islands.

She has found her on Twitter! Her fingers clack excitedly. The opening message is sent. Staring deep into the glowing screen, she waits for her to respond. She doesn't have to wait long. The exchange begins. For each question there's a reply and I feel more and more alone as she disappears into their dialogue. During the briefest of pauses, she chugs down her entire dinner juice in one go and smashes the glass between her fingers. I get the antibacterial wipes and the plasters. As I'm mopping up the blood, I tell her I think she's more beautiful now than she's ever been, but too sore for sex, apparently.

Saturday

I GET UP before my time and watch her getting ready in the bathroom. Stood in front of the mirror, she slicks up her body with melted shea butter, it resembles umbilical fluid, like she is being reborn. Splashed shea butter is hardening around the tap and against the mirror where it escaped her and I allow myself a frown – it will be me that has to chisel it off later. Applying blusher across her red cheeks she says, miserably, 'I feel like I'm polishing a turd.'

I tell her this is almost over. Her body's the most cleansed in the country, 'probably the world!' With a *whoosh* and a *click* she closes the door on me. It's now her 'private time'. I make the bed and sweep the dry skin off the bed sheets. I wonder whether, if I begin to save the skin waiting for me every morning, I could stitch together another version of her. It could be her companion, one that understands what she's going through and can keep her company through 'private time'.

Walking into town I see her, unexpectedly. She's

standing in the middle of the pavement, shoulders hunched, a hand outstretched, as if trying to reach something just below her waist. I check my watch. Her work began thirty-five minutes ago. I very carefully put my hands on her shoulders, she stiffens, but is too tired to be surprised.

'There was a husky,' she says.

'That's nice,' I reply. She allows me to walk her to the door of her work.

'I'm hungry,' she pleads.

That night she looks at her dinner juice as if I've poisoned it. I have trout, with garlic and chilli kale. I feel more than gluttonous.

Sunday

I WAKE IN the middle of the night, sitting up against the headboard. I don't know what wakes me, instinctively I look sideways. The top of her head is poking out from the duvet, hair splayed across the pillow like a desert spider waiting for its web to snag. A soft ethereal glow permeates the space around her. The soft *tap, tap, tap,* of keys being lovingly struck, reaches my ears. I know who she's talking to. And I know she answers her prayers.

It's Sunday and I drag her through the market – a place we frequented before all of this – but she looks at me like she doesn't know me anymore. We perform an open-air domestic whilst buying succulents. I'll admit it, I falter. It's a mumbled comment after a fair question. This is now everything to her. It's not just these seven days, it's a complete change of lifestyle. It's for the rest of her life.

The rest of her life.

Monday

AND ON THE seventh day … Alleluia! The Cleansing's working! Patches of snow coloured skin, floating upon lava. I tell her I can see them. She laughs out loud, takes photos of her legs, arms and tummy and posts them online, taping out at least ten inches of blurb to accompany each one. I'm happy too – happy she's happy.

Around two o'clock I slump out of a long meeting and check my phone—twenty-six missed calls. They're all from her. I try calling back. It doesn't go through, almost as if she's out of range. The day outside is bright and warm but there's a big black cloud approaching the city. Inside the cloud I can see electricity charging.

I call her work. Eventually I get one of her colleges. She says she left hours ago because of stomach problems. 'Is she okay?' she whispers into the phone, concerned. Apparently everyone at work has noticed a 'severe change' in her. Providing a vague response, I hang up. Making my excuses I leave work an hour and a half early. As I remove my coat from the back of my chair, the one colleague of mine I've spoken to about her Cleansing raises his eyebrows. 'Better you than me,' he says, unhelpfully.

As I walk home the storm cloud blocks out the sun and the world loses lumens. Fat, heavy drops begin to stain my jacket, but I just about make it beneath the house's awning before the heavens open. Our little carpark and the road beyond come alive with the sound of water smashing upon it. Breathing deeply, I steady myself.

The smells of curry, toast and something sweet being baked in the other flats, greets me as I open the door and begin to climb the stairs. When I reach my door, it's already ajar. A thin coil of silver mist laps at the welcome mat. The plastic cover for the electric metre has steamed over. Inside my flat, I can barely see two foot in front of me. Our little corridor resembles a World War I trench, all that's missing is the sound of gun fire. Instead there's only the *drip, drip, drip,* of a tap. The bathroom door's open – that's the source of the steam. When I go to push the door open fully, I see my hand shaking. I can't figure why.

The bathroom window's closed. Frosted light struggles to hit the edge of the bathtub, where a red hand rests. I whisper her name into the mist. The hand doesn't twitch. For some reason I don't go to her immediately, I move past and slide the window open. Gradually, the mist disperses, enough that I can see her shape filling the bathtub. Red has enveloped her entire body. Almost as if she's been pulled inside out. Her ankles and her arms are braced, as if she was trying to escape something. But her eyes are closed. She looks peaceful.

Reaching out, I lightly grip her shoulders. Skin folds beneath my fingers like wet cardboard. A split appears down the centre of her body and a tongue of silver steam escapes near her collar bone. I step back. Her body sags. The edges of the split no longer match up. One half of her is lower than the other. I reach out to ... reseal her, but before I can make contact, the seam bursts with a hiss. Steam rushes over my hands. I retract, scolded, and fall onto the toilet seat.

The head crumples inwards. The cocoon deflates. With a slurp it slumps over, and slides below the water.

I hit the corridor wall, hand over mouth; I think I'm going to vomit. I try to take breaths that would fill a paper bag and collapse onto my knees. There are footprints on the carpet; fresh ones. Out the corner of my eye I see movement in the living room. Although the rain's heavier than ever, sunlight pours in through the windows, bleaching the mist that hovers around the silhouette of a figure stood in the centre of the room, looking out. With difficulty I manage to swallow whatever was about to make its resurrection and stand up straight. It's whispering to itself.

I approach, swiping at the air. The clouds disburse enough that I think I see her face. But that's impossible.

'Don't worry. It's all natural,' she says, dressed all in white, smooth white skin beneath bouncy blonde curls. She looks like an angel. I whisper something to console her, but she's already beaming. It's a smile that says, everything's going to be alright.

It's Not Normal to Befriend a Trapped Butterfly

Emily Harrison

YOU FIND THE butterfly trapped inside the double-glazing of Sam's bedroom window. Its delicate wings are fanned out, as though stuck in mid-flight, and its colour – burnt orange bordered in black – is neatly symmetrical.

It wasn't there the night before, when you'd gone in to close the curtains, was it?

'Hello,' you whisper. 'How'd you get there?'

There's no hole in Sam's window. No crack in the wood that could be wide enough. Up close it reminds you of the amber fossils your Nan used to have lined up on the oak console in her cottage. She'd let you rearrange them, if you asked nicely.

With your hand outstretched and the slight paunch of your stomach pushing against the jut of the sill, you press a finger to the glass and tap. You expect nothing. It's just a curious attempt at touch. But like magic, the butterfly's wings ripple.

***

SHE CALLS JUST after lunch and tells you she's coming by to collect some of her things: a vinyl collection, several boxes of dog-eared books, a suitcase full of photos she wants. You've stacked it all in piles in the narrow hallway.

There's another voice on the line, bleeding in behind hers. It asks about timings and whether they should 'Stay in the car, would that be for the best?'

You wonder who the voice belongs to. You're not surprised she's found someone new. It's her M.O when things get hard: new friends, new clothes, new lover? It's different this time. The inexplicable thing that split you apart isn't a blip or an argument or a flaw in the infrastructure of you and her. There can be no U-turn from the inexplicable thing. It doesn't work like that.

***

SAM'S ROOM OVERLOOKS a street of tightly packed terrace houses with white sash windows. You wait at his window until she arrives, watching the butterfly in its sentient state. You still can't figure out how it got there.

Down below, a car pulls up. A 4X4 with snow on the roof rack. It's been snowing since the turn of the year. Falling in palm sized clumps. She gets out at the passenger side – long legs, broad shoulders. Her cherry red Dr

Martens sink into the grey slush that lines the kerb. The driver stays put. You can just make out a hand on the steering wheel, holding it loose.

Is it Lee, the woman she trains with at the gym? You know she fancies her. She fancies a lot of people.

'It's natural', she used to say, 'to find people attractive.'

You never disputed it. You let her have her fancies.

***

'YOU ALRIGHT?' SHE asks, after she's put her things in the boot of the car. Her cheeks are speckled in red. Instead of helping, you sat on the bottom step of the stairs and let her lug the boxes on her own. A small, empty victory.

'Yeah. Fine.'

There was a time, before the separation, before the inexplicable thing, when you would say 'Fine', and she would say 'Nobody is just fine.'

But she just nods.

'I'll pick up the last of my things next week. Maybe Tuesday. I should have the keys to my flat by then.'

Will she come and pick you up too, amongst her shirts that are still in the wardrobe and the mountain bike that's still locked up in the shed? You used to be one of her things. Her everything, if you're going to get sentimental about it.

She lingers. Her eyes rove from you to the top of the

stairs, kitchen, front room and back again. You want to ask if there's anything else? Any room she'd like to go in? She hasn't gone beyond shuffling back and forth along the hallway, leaving wet boot prints on the wood. Hasn't taken the stairs and ventured to your bedroom where you lay together beneath crisp sheets. Where you drank strawberry, mint and chamomile tea and she read library-loaned books, and together you lounged in the lull of late weeknights, equally worn with work. Where you cradled Sam and absorbed his adoring eyes, wide as the cosmos. Where she decided – or was it you? – that in the after-math of the inexplicable thing, it was time to not do this anymore. This being marriage. Unity. Co-existing inside a house that she'd wanted, and you hadn't.

She hasn't crossed the landing either. Hasn't stepped over the threshold and into Sam's room. She hasn't been in it since she left. You have, every day, tidying clothes, toys, keepsakes, that don't need to be tidied and inhaling his scent on his perfectly made bedsheets. Soap and talc. You don't want to call her a coward. She's allowed to be scared.

'Is that Lee?' you ask, as you show her out of her own house.

'Yes.'

'Oh.'

'I can ex—'

'There's a butterfly trapped inside Sam's bedroom

window,' you say, and close the door before she has chance to reply.

***

THE INEXPLICABLE THING is this: your two-year-old boy who barrelled around like his body was constantly brand new and the world – sea, sky, the snails on the path and the slugs in the garden – was an unending marvel, was struck by an elderly woman doing 30 miles per hour in a 20 zone.

Of all the things you can recall of that day, it's the elderly woman's diluted milk-blue eyes and how she doddered over to you as though one leg was shorter than the other.

'I'm sorry for your loss', people would say, in the hours, days, weeks, months after, their arms laden with tray bakes of flapjacks and brownies and soon-to-be binned carnations.

It never felt like a loss. It felt like what it was: a cataclysm that had shifted the foundations on which you'd built yourself, your love, your life.

'I'm sorry you're no longer the person you were before', they should have said. 'I'm sorry you're an outline now. I'm sorry your relationship was never made to withstand the inexplicable.'

Sorry. Sorry. Sorry.

***

SHE IS ALONE on Tuesday morning and the car is hers this time.

She heads for the kitchen and makes a black coffee for herself and a chamomile tea for you. You don't want to give her credit for stepping beyond the hallway this time.

'What did you mean about the butterfly?' she asks. She takes a sip from her cup and squeezes her eyes shut.

You tell her, again, that it's trapped inside Sam's bedroom window.

'Is it a joke?'

'Why would I joke?' There's little to joke about anymore.

'Can I go up and see it?'

You stand side-by-side at the window. You can tell by her silence that she's confused.

'How did it get there?'

You shrug.

'How is it not dead?'

You're not sure of that, either.

'You'd think it would be, considering how long it's been there.'

You think so, too.

Before she leaves, she sets her hand on your forearm.

'Might be time for us to empty his room?'

There is no 'us' about it.

***

YOU'VE BEGUN TALKING to the butterfly. Between answering work calls and filling in budget spend spreadsheets, you take your tea and marmalade-smothered toast, or mid-afternoon white wine and Greek salad, and weave stories about your life: a childhood broken arm (double fracture); the night you did ecstasy (one to forget); Paris, when she proposed (one to remember). You hang them like spider silk.

You talk to Sam sometimes too. You curl up on his bed, push your face against the dinosaur print duvet, and tell him how missing him is a wound that won't heal. The white C-section that puckers from your skin. The way it undulates. A near constant sting.

***

IT'S THE FIRST anniversary.

You are bound to her by this bereavement. You will never not have it. You could reach the end of the universe where atoms are ripped apart into nothingness and your life will still dovetail into hers.

She calls early and after a series of mundane questions, you tell her your parents visited the day before. You tell her you told them you want to be alone.

'Are they there now?'

Her voice lilts. You picture her bottom lip worrying

between her front teeth.

'They went home this morning,' you reply.

She is silent. She was silent when the inexplicable thing happened. A mute for days.

You prop yourself against the window and gaze at the butterfly as she breathes down the line. What would be like to touch its wings? Delicate. Soft. So easy to break.

Her quiet grows, and you consider bringing up the butterfly, just to rupture it.

She sighs.

'I don't know what to say.'

What is there to say?

Right before she hangs up, you tell her that missing Sam is like wearing a weighted vest of grief. When the line goes dead, you tell the black screen of your phone that you might miss her. The safety she brought. The surety of her in your home.

***

WINTER HANDS THE reins to spring and the sky becomes less bruised.

It's been five weeks since you last laid eyes on her. Her and Lee are girlfriend and girlfriend now. Facebook official. You could be happy for her, if you tried.

Still, the space she occupies inside of your life results in sending her arbitrary texts. More often than not, she asks about the butterfly. You explain that it's still there.

You reveal that it has become something you can rely upon, even if it's just its existence alone. When you tell her that you're sure it has begun to talk – broken sentences, clips of words, concrete nouns – she replies:

Her: I'm worried about you.

You: Why?

Her: I just am.

The three dots appear. Type. Type. Type.

Her: I think you might need help.

You: Help?

Her: It's not normal to befriend a trapped butterfly. Let alone talk to one.

You: It's fine.

Her: It's not though, is it?

You don't reply. You don't want to admit that she might be right.

***

IT'S ALMOST MIDNIGHT and you're cross-legged on the soft carpet of Sam's bedroom floor. Behind you, cast in the pearl moonlight, the butterfly's wings *tsk tsk tsk* between the glass panes.

Tiredness has pawed at you since you ate your dinner while watching the 10 o'clock news, but rather than give in, you've spent the past hour alternating between mouthfuls of dessert wine and clicking through web articles on your phone.

After the 'Which Disney Princess Are You?' article (Rapunzel, apparently) and one that explains how seahorses are monogamous for life, you click on one titled '10 Things I Love About You.' The article is a spin on a film you watched as a teen and a song you haven't heard of. It asks you to see if you can list the ten things you love about your partner. It claims it's 'Just for fun.' You don't want fun, but you need a something that isn't sleep and the way your dreams are spliced with visions of Sam. Pure spectral punishment.

Ten things? You open up the Notes app and speak aloud so the butterfly can join in.

'That she was nice?'

The butterfly hums. You turn and smile.

'Generous?'

'You can do better than that.'

'That she was good looking?'

The butterfly says you're being vague. Eventually you type:

1. The slope of her spine and how she would purr like a cat when I scratched my fingers down it.

2. Her unapologetic acceptance of her sexuality, and her unwavering support when I was so scared of mine.

3. Her ability to build things.

The fourth and fifth feel surface level though you type them anyway.

4. How she slept with the curtains open because she said it was the only way to let the stars in.
5. Her talent for boiling the perfect dippy egg.

A sixth?
'That she knew how to kiss?'
'Bit boring.'

So did Craig, your secondary school boyfriend who had a collection of ant-like blackheads tucked in the crease of his chin.

You wonder if you loved her because she was there. There's a lot to be said for being real and bound by gravity.

The next few points come in a rush and you fail to make it to ten.

6. Her unwavering joy whenever she was holding Sam.
7. I don't know. I just did.
8. Because she loved me.

***

NUMBER THREE PLAYS on your mind. Building. Maybe she's doing that now. Maybe she's putting up shelves to prop framed photos of her and Lee on. They went to Paris last week. A mid-April weekend away. You saw it on Instagram. Lee on her arm, all blonde and picture perfect and in the place where she'd proposed to you.

Does she ever think of Sam?

Maybe she's screwing together bits of IKEA furniture for the new house they might be getting. She can't stay in her one bed flat forever, can she?

Maybe they're just screwing each other.

With bare feet you tiptoe across the dewy grass towards the lopsided ochre playhouse that has morphed into a shed. You fiddle the key in the rusted padlock until it clicks open. Her tools are there, laid out across the metal workbench that's gathering dust. A hammer, a box of screwdrivers, nails, some wrenches and bits you can't put a name to. Her mountain bike is still chained up, webs knotting around the handlebars.

You pick up the hammer and let the weight of it take your arm. The handle is wooden and splattered in green paint. You recall her using it in the garden, rebuilding the fence after a summer storm had pulled it from the soil. Sam was six months old then. Precious and dainty and substantial and plentiful. He weighed the world and weighed nothing at all.

You leave the rest and carry the hammer into your home.

***

THE HAMMER HAS resided on the breakfast table for a week. The weather hasn't been right for what you've decided to do. Deluges of fat rain. But today is different. Today is faultless blue.

In a sure grip, you take the hammer and make for Sam's bedroom, sidestepping the unopened mail that's addressed to her in the hallway and the piles of washing strewn across the landing.

'Hello,' you say to the butterfly as you ease open Sam's door. The hinges give a tired creak.

'Hello,' the butterfly says back, its voice symphonic.

The hammer is heavy in your hand, the metal head resting cold against your thigh. You pad over to the window and set your index finger to the top left corner.

'Come up here', you say. 'Right up. I don't want you to get hurt.'

It shuffles. Stops. You inhale. Count backwards. Three. Two. One.

You smash the hammer straight through the window. You swing with so much force your arm follows, shards of glass splintering into your skin. The butterfly screams and you suck the sides of your cheeks between your teeth at the sight of the blood prickling up like uncanny polka dots. Remember the cut you gave yourself when you were fourteen just to see what the sensation would feel like.

Remember Sam on the side of the road?

You swing again. And again. Slugging until all that's left is a single shard where the butterfly screeches.

'No. No! Shhh. Don't be scared.'

Sam was scared of dogs, thunder, the dark. He'd cry in the night and you'd go running every time.

You drop the hammer and reach out to touch the butterfly. It arcs away.

'It's time for you to go.'

Is it? Are you sure? You could carry it with you. You could tuck it deep and safe in bags, coats, pockets. It could flutter around Sam's room. You could cherish it, forever, like a child.

After several seconds of silence, it speaks.

'What about you?'

The question mars.

'Me? I'll be fine. I might come too.'

Your serrated arm is throbbing, and the butterfly is stalling. Wide-eyed. Unsure. Clinging.

You don't want to cry. Not at this.

Its wings tilt. *Tsk. Tsk.* The burnt orange catches the morning light that they're near crystalline as it floats out of the window frame. You've yet to see the butterfly soar. It loops up and suspends itself as though it's held on an invisible puppet string.

On the street below, a man with plump Pitbull on a leash, and a mouth like a gaping carp, waves his arms as though he's taxiing a plane.

'Oi!'

With wobbling hands, you grip the sides of the glass-less window frame and round up a leg, climbing until you're half in, half out. The dog barks and he shouts: 'What the fuck are you doing?'

What are you doing? The window, the blood, the butterfly. You don't know how to pick these pieces apart because you'd planned this far but what next? Maybe you could call her from up here. Your phone is in your pocket. She might run red lights and take the stairs two at a time until she can pull you from the ledge and tell you that this is what happens when you bury grief. She might say that she knows Sam is this room. This house. The first thing in the morning and the last thing at night.

She'd probably just call for an ambulance.

The spring air slips around you, stirring your skin, filling your lungs. The scent of fresh cut grass seeps.

You pitch to the side. Drown out the voice of the passer by whose yelling that he's worried for your safety. He needn't be. The softness of Sam's carpet will break your fall.

Flash Fiction Judge's Report – Susmita Bhattacharya

FIRST PRIZE: APPLE-FALL
BY JASON JACKSON
Susmita said: I loved the sweeping saga of Catherine's life – from her childhood with her grandmother, picking apples, pushing boundaries, discovering herself, loving and losing loved ones to becoming childlike again in her last years – all these observations and experiences so heartrendingly portrayed in so few words.

SECOND PRIZE: THE WEIGHT OF FEATHERS
BY REBECCA KELLY
Susmita said: This had such strong imagery. The metaphor of the owl's wings imprinting its presence on the narrator and the guilt and grief carried on those young shoulders made me stop and consider the weight that the story carried on its slim shoulders.

THIRD PRIZE: VISITING HOURS
BY E. E. RHODES
Susmita said: *Visiting Hours* had a mythical feel to it. I loved the lyrical quality of the story, the back and forth of

questions with so many layers to it. In the midst of the poetic language is a stark truth that defines the relationship between the two characters in the story.

HIGHLY COMMENDED: HOW TO MAKE DAMSON JAM BY NATALIE QUINN

Susmita said: I loved the recipe format. On the surface it tells the steps to make a good damson jam. On another level, there is something else going on. Relationships are tested. Life's lessons are learned. A quiet story bursting with the richness of sensory detail and layered meaning.

Flash Fiction First Prize

Apple-fall

Jason Jackson

Harvest

CATHERINE'S GRANDMOTHER KEEPS an orchard, and each year they pick apples together. The kitchen cupboard is a dark space with wooden slats where the apples rest. *If they don't touch, they'll last into spring,* her grandmother says, leaning in, setting them down. Catherine thinks about the apples as she lies awake in bed. She thinks about the spaces between them. One night, she creeps downstairs and opens the cupboard, breathing in the cloying sweetness of the fruit. She reaches as far as she can, takes hold of an apple, moves it to rest against another. In the morning, she hides beneath the bedsheets and listens to her grandmother singing downstairs.

Seed

LONDON, JANUARY. SHE'S twenty-one. Her rented flat is

cold, the boiler broken. The streets are filled with strangers. She takes her book to the pub, hides in the corner by the fire. The man says his name is Richard. *D'ya want to play darts?* It's ridiculous, her aim appalling, but he throws with a calm, hypnotic rhythm. *You're good*, she says, and he smiles. Afterwards, she holds him close in her freezing bed, watching his sleeping breath drift away from her own.

Roots

SHE NAMES HER son Nicholas, but he is always Nick. A strong boy, he dwarfs her by the time he reaches his teens. Sometimes, she'll be at the sink with the dishes and he'll take each plate, each mug, dry them and put them away. On the nights she can't sleep, she goes to his darkened room and watches him, the space between them heavy with her love. When he's seventeen, a building job comes up in another town. *Jamie says we can stay with his mate at first.* She kisses him on the doorstep, his friends waiting in the car, and that night in the living room she watches as the flames burn logs to embers. In the morning she takes ash from the grate, rubs it on her breasts, her belly, her thighs, making of herself a small, grey ghost.

Blight

HER NAME IS Rachel, and they stay in his old room when

they visit. The bed's too small, but Nick just laughs. *We can snuggle up in here together fine.* Catherine lies awake in bed, trying not to listen, remembering how it felt: winter in London with someone to hold. Nick likes to say, *you're beautiful, Mum. Still young.* But she isn't. And now there's something silent and rotten in her bones, in her blood. *He loves you,* she says to Rachel, as if it's a curse. *You'll never make him happy.* During the last days, Nick comes to the hospital, sits in the chair, cries. She wants to say, *climb up here next to me and we'll sleep,* but the white of the room takes her words, and at night she dreams of apple-fall, the flesh of them still firm, still sweet.

Flash Fiction Second Prize
The Weight of Feathers
Rebecca Netley

SOMETIME DURING THE night an owl hit the glass and left the ghost-like pattern of its wings. The glass did not fall, but fissured and spangled making prisms of sun on the tiles.

Through the window, my children's movements fracture in the pane's flaws. I remember my brother Roddy in his shorts, knees as big as cooking apples and I, in the too-tight dresses, lying on the yellowed grass listening to laughter from other gardens.

Our fence had holes and I spent hours peering onto the house at the back where the Miller family lived. It was in the spring that Buster came to them, sun-coloured fur and paws like a lion. The children tumbled over him while Mr and Mrs Miller looked on smiling. I marvelled at the lolling tongue, the way Buster rolled onto his back. I imagined burying my head into his coat. 'Over here, Buster,' the Miller children called, 'Come on boy, come on. Good boy.'

We saw them on those silent Sunday walks to church, the pavement stirring dust beneath my best shoes. Roddy with his face scrubbed so red you couldn't see the tears. 'Leave the dog,' my mother said, and I could only watch as they passed.

The hard pews. My father pressed too close in his shiny suit and my mother rapt as she knelt for communion, but we had been happy, hadn't we, returning home to the smell of roast meat?

'Thank you, Mummy. It's delicious,' we said and hoped for a scrap of rapture to return to her gaze. Outside, Buster barking.

'Bloody dog,' my father said.

Don't bark again, I would think, don't bark, but on Buster went as we cringed in our seats until my father slammed the table. The crash of the back door.

'Shut that thing up!' And I thought of the little ones holding balls out in their palms.

'Eat up,' I say now as Molly picks at her food, 'It's your favourite.'

And later I cannot remember if that's true. It begins to rain and the cracks in the glass divert the drops like railway points.

After Buster died, an owl began to call behind our houses. I opened the window and willed it to sit at the foot of my bed in the bristling dark. The sound of a flush at the end of the corridor and someone crying.

I think of Buster now, long dead. How Mrs Miller held the children, arms tight about them like wings.

'That'll teach them,' my father said, hands on the fork, his secret triumph gleaming like a pearl in his iris. We all knew. And I had pressed the lamb to my lips to the choke of horror.

I still wake sometimes, wake to the sound of Buster barking and then, in the silence, a flutter of feather. I imagine myself deeper into the moment until finally, it presses its wings across my back, leaving the imprint of someone else's distant embrace.

Flash Fiction Third Prize

Visiting Hours

E.E. Rhodes

…..

…..

'Are you my wife?' my husband said to me.

'No, I'm a mermaid and I've brought you a gift.'

And he took the cockled seashells from me with a sliding smile and held one up to his ear and listened.

'It's the sea, all trapped and stormed,' he said, surprised again, and then looked inside it and showed me.

And he got angry sometimes in this antiseptic striped and green place, so all I could do was nod at him to agree.

…..

……

'Are you my sister?' my husband said to me.

'No, I'm an albatross on the wing, coming in soon.'

And he frowned and then held out a broad hand, whitened at the knuckles and missing half a fish-hooked finger.

'May I have a feather, then, to save our souls?' he asked, as though it wasn't another broken thing we told between us.

And I promised I'd bring him one, if I could climb his rope lined cliff-face, the next time I came.

.....

.....

'Are you my mother?' my husband said to me.

'No, I'm a selkie, with my skin blanket for you.'

And there was the old fear at the corner of his eyes, in the creases. Something sharp and drowned remembered.

'And will you keep us warm?' he said, as though I had never covered him before.

And I gave him a fur rug that he smoothed down uneasily until it hung, regretted, in folds over his knees.

.....

.....

'Are you my daughter?' my husband said to me.

'No, I'm a place in the summerlands where she's waiting for you patiently.'

And I thought of our child that the doctors speared out of me, slipped as she was with our mixing gone sour.

'She should have taken after me,' he said, with rheumy, nodded, knit-bone knowing, each part of us unmoored.

And I made us both our tea, and he drank it from the saucer, and there was no reason now to scold him.

.....

.....

'Are you my wife?' my husband said to me.

'No, I'm your widow.'

And I knew that he was trying for the name of us. But we have never been that easy.

'I never should have married you,' he muttered, more

salty lucid now than either of us have ever been.

And in this slow progression of lines unravelling every day is different, and like the tide with what it brings, also always the tedious salt burned same.

.....
.....

Flash Fiction Highly Commended

How to Make Damson Jam

Morgan Quinn

1. Find a tree to forage from. The fruit are at their best in Autumn, straining at the branches like weighted bruises. When you spot the perfect tree on your way to school, map its location carefully in your mind's eye. There won't be time to stop as Mam will be pulling you along, her heels clip-clipping the pavement, her head full of Important Things, her sparkly nails pinching your wrists.

2. It is best to go damson picking with Grandma. She will listen quietly and help you draw a map to the tree's location. She will have a wicker basket to collect the fruits. She will balance it in the crook of her arm. Her nails will be clipped and uniform. They won't damage the fruit. She will hold your hand and her skin will be as soft and smooth as a ripe tomato.

3. Don't eat the fruit raw. They are tart, sour. They will make you wrinkle your nose, suck in your cheeks and

purse your lips. It is the face Mam makes when you ask her to sign your reading record for school. It is the face Grandma makes when Mam drops you on her doorstep in your thin cotton pyjamas and winter boots.

4. A damson is a clingstone fruit. You will need to remove the stone with a sharp knife. It won't want to leave but you must persist. A swift, clean cut is best.

5. Choose a heavy pan. A pan that takes two hands and all your strength to lift. Put your damsons in the pan with some water. Turn up the heat and watch the damsons dance and bounce and shudder as they try to escape. Think of Mam, her eyes painted like purple plums, twirling around the apartment with the man who isn't your father.

6. Pour in sugar. Golden granulated is best. Watch it dissolve as you stir. It will disappear like magic, the last hints of gold vanishing into nothingness. It will look like the setting sun did, shimmering off Mam's hair as you watched her walk away. The sugar is still there. You just can't see it anymore.

7. Once the mixture is boiling, you must leave it alone. Look away. Ignore it. Pretend you don't see it until the crucial moment. Then, if you want it to set properly, you must lavish your attention upon it. Stir gently, but thoroughly.

8. Don't decant into jars too quickly. Leave it to settle first. Jam doesn't like upheaval. If you move it too soon, all the plump fruit, the sweetness, the goodness will sink to the bottom and be lost.

9. If your jars were sterile, and you sealed them properly, your jam will last for a long time. Maybe years. Write Mam's name on a label, and put it in the fridge for when she comes to take you home.

10. Don't ask Grandma the question. Swallow it down with a spoonful of delicious damson jam.

Fledgling

Rae Cowie

HE FLAPPED LIKE litter; papery wings fluttering amongst the gravel of the verge, hopping awkwardly towards the blackened dandelions and sluggish ditch water. She was so certain she had crushed him; made him another piece of forgotten roadkill. Just another sad event in a crap day … a crap week … a crap month. But instead of being frightened, his blinking eyes shone moist, curious. Their inky softness innocent, like her son's, as the crow swivelled his smooth head, following her movements. He must surely be young. She checked the surrounding undergrowth. Was his mum tucked somewhere safe, within the thickets of grass? Watching?

On the opposite side of the road stood a sprawling ash, its branches heavy with foliage. Was there a nest hidden high amongst the scramble of leaves? But crows were noisy birds that roosted in groups. She had listened to a podcast where a woman enthused about how intelligent, how sociable a species they were. And now she had gone and hurt one. Would he be missed? Was he longing for his mum?

She waited a second before kneeling and slowly reaching out a hand. Her fingers trembled as she stroked his fluffy wing, which felt downy as catkins, that lay twisted at a clumsy angle. Was it broken? Would it fix? Cool sunlight lanced his head feathers, making their smoky tips gleam, as a luminous mayfly skittered amongst the weeds at his side. The chick chirped.

She couldn't leave him.

He felt unbearably light as she scooped his faint warmth between her cupped palms. Instinctively he pecked and nipped, drawing a speckle of blood from her thumb. The violent patter of his heart matched the rhythm of her own. Slimy olive shit slid between her fingers and landed with a splat, messing her white trainers. It didn't matter. They would wash.

She edged backwards, cooing to him as she nudged open the door of her jeep and set him into the shallow dip of the baby car seat. The fleece blanket she tucked around him still smelled of milk and talcum. She planned on warming some sugared water and feeding him from a teaspoon – a tip she had gleaned from the podcast, one she never imagined she would need.

Gently, she shut the door and rounded the vehicle, wiping her hands against her jeans before she slipped into the driver's side, checking the backseat in the mirror, a habit she had yet to unlearn. The bird glanced about him inquisitively, silent. Seemingly happy enough to trust her. Her throat thickened with tenderness. She hadn't meant to hurt him. Her mind had been elsewhere. She would take him to the vet's, but what if his wing wouldn't heal?

Her breasts ached with fullness as her nipples tingled and her t-shirt grew damp. Not again. She gripped the steering wheel, tethering herself as she bowed her head, breathing deeply to contain the grief she felt—for the bird, for her son, for herself.

The Circular Trajectories of Drones

Jan Kaneen

HAVE YOU SLICED the beans? Have you seasoned the meat? Have you cleaned the pan beside the bread machine?

On he rattles with his head-chef questions. He could be saying anything for all I care, or chanting the same-old thing again and again, because there's nowhere to go and no-one to see and nothing to do but pointless preparation on this flat and futile Sunday afternoon. Well this sous-chef wife ain't for listening. She's drifting off.

By the time I've floated up to the ceiling his words are a distant drone – meaningless consonants, hollow and empty. I gaze below me, marvelling at how different everything looks from up here – the cooker, the sink – as flat as photos. I call down to tell him, but my tongue is cold and sharp and there's a strange metallic taste in my mouth. I wave to get his attention and feel myself lurching sideward. That's when I realise. I'm not floating, but hovering. I process the change and recalibrate, assessing my new appendages, and am surprised to find I know all their names: a canopy to protect my motor, propellers to keep me air-born, landing skids for if I ever decide to return to earth. I focus my wireless-receptors and tune into my husband.

'Have you sliced the beans? Have you seasoned the meat? Have you cleaned the pan beside the bread machine?'

I feel strangely calm because he hasn't changed, and whizz round the lampshade to hone my skills, zooming and swooping in the spacious inside. Why have I never noticed how high and wide the kitchen is? I drop myself into his personal airspace, spinning my blades just millimetres from his face. He doesn't look up, he carries on cooking and chopping and chanting. I'm not irritated. His sameness feels like safety, freedom even, and gives me courage. I dart up to the half-open skylight where my sharp edges catch the frail sunlight, then I glide outside.

'Today is only mine,' I call in my new tinny voice because he deserves the truth after 30 years of marriage. And that's when he looks up – his face all vowels – wide-open Os, his mouth, his eyes, his upturned head, tipped back in circular surprise. I feel a pang of sadness for him, anchored as he is on the heavy earth where he's always, always been.

By suppertime I'm exhausted and buzz back home. I've travelled countryside and conurbations; motorways and parks; skimmed the surface of rivers and turbulent seas – all dull and distant like dreary maps of themselves. He's sitting waiting at the table that's neatly laid for two. I hang over his right shoulder to decompress, and he plugs me in to recharge my batteries. I can't actually smell his human food yet, but I'm close enough to process that the beans have been sautéed very gently, that the fresh-baked bread is melting the butter, that the meat has been cooked for hours-and-hours until it's deliciously, achingly soft and tender.

Baggage

Charlie Swailes

WHEN NO ONE else was in the house, I would visit the suitcase my mother kept in the back of her wardrobe. I would push aside her dresses and coats, feel the softness of silk, the tickle of fur until I found it, pale blue and hard-shelled.

I was six when I first found it, hiding from one of my father's rages. Her clothes were delicately placed: thin top, thick jumper, pyjamas, underwear. A bag of toiletries. An envelope of cash. A list of phone numbers. Fear scratched up my throat as I realised what this was. She was leaving. She had had enough knocks and blows and was leaving me. Leaving me with him. I buried my hands in the neat folds of her clothes trying to claw her back to me.

But then I saw it. A chunk of bright yellow among her greys and blues. I reached in and pulled out the woollen socks thought I had lost many weeks ago. Here they were, in her suitcase. I dug deeper. Thin tops, thick jumpers, new pyjamas, still in their plastic wrap. And below that, colouring books; fat, bright crayons, fresh in the box.

I was coming too.

When I next saw her, I told her. Not with my words but with my eyes. They looked at her clearing ash spilt from my father's snoring cigarette hand and told her I had found it. They watched her serving peas under the barrage of abuse, spit and hate and told her I was excited to leave. They locked onto her face as she applied makeup to a blossoming purple bruise that matched one on my arm and said, I love you.

But the bruise turned black, then blue, then yellow. And the suitcase remained in the wardrobe.

Seasons crept along. The clothes in the suitcase changed periodically. The amount of cash fluctuated. The clothes for me changed from dresses and ankle socks, to jeans and hooded tops. From frilly child's knickers emblazoned with cartoon characters, to training bras in muted colours. From picture books to teen magazines. Still I visited, curled up in the dim light and sifted gently through the contents, feeling the soft cottons as hugs my mother couldn't openly bestow upon me.

And then, quite unexpectedly, I was gone. The suitcase, nestled in the back of the wardrobe as it always was, contained only my mother's clothes. I searched to the bottom, digging down pulling out piece after piece but found only her. I had been ejected, cast out of the plan. Whenever she was going, she now intended to go alone.

That evening she smiled at me: a warm, loving smile that stopped just before it reached her eyes. I looked away.

That night, I packed my own suitcase.

Homemaker

Dan Micklethwaite

JADE TOOK THE chainsaw to her new husband's torso, then to his shoulders, then to his head. With the wreck of her old marriage festering, tender, she followed this up with the chisel and rasp; with sandpaper swabbed at the grazes and cuts. Repeated the act on her three brand-new children, two sons and a daughter. Brushed on the varnish and left them to dry.

It was only that evening, with the oak statues seated around the ash table, that she began to feel calmer. Nestled down in her chair with a bottle of red.

It didn't really matter who'd cheated on whom, or who'd had the best, most expensive attorney. Didn't matter that she had been called a bad wife – let alone a bad mother – or that her art, for so long, had been misunderstood.

That belonged to the past, to be swept up and disposed of like the afternoon's sawdust, and the offcuts of lumber she'd fed to the stove. They crackled and popped like November the fifth, or the echoes of faraway mortars and guns.

She toasted her recent escape from that conflict; held her new husband's gaze as she clinked with his glass. Was entranced by those eyes and the set of his jawline, and the way they had both been passed on to the kids. A true model family. It was all that she'd wanted.

She drank, and desisted from further inspection.

She did not want to risk finding knots in the grain.

2084

Pete Barnes

NEXT TO A bend in the Thames, in a field called 'Royal National Theatre', a robin searches for worms in the soil that is disturbed each time Millicent pulls a carrot from the ground. Every now and then the bird flutters within a yard of her hand, tilts its head and chirps expectantly. In response, the young woman playfully tilts her own head, and attempts a few chirps of reply. In the next field, 'Hayward Gallery', Millicent's uncles pick strawberries, laughing and chatting while red admirals flip flop around them in the late afternoon sun.

As far as she can see there are green fields, orchards of pink apples, and scattered copses where badgers and hedgehogs slumber until darkness comes. And just over the water at 'Embankment Station', she can hear school children singing *Frère Jacques* among red current bushes that thrive where passing trains once shook the ground.

Other than the little school and the handful of modest homes scattered about it, the only man-made structure she can see is the towering, shimmering Monument. Spearing three hundred meters from its base in 'Pudding Lane' meadows, the white needle's elegant form is entirely unbroken, except for a black crown that encircles its upper reaches, just beneath where the hypodermic tip threatens to puncture a cyan sky.

Though Millicent does not realise it, the crown is in fact a dense nest of cameras, microphones, transmitters and sensors of every kind – all ceaselessly, monitoring, gauging, checking … and thinking. After a picosecond's consideration, the Monument may determine, for example, that sufficient root vegetables have been harvested, or that enough time has been spent learning French. In which case it simply and silently diverts resources towards some other objective.

At the 'Royal National Theatre', Millicent looks with satisfaction at the twelve sacks of carrots she has filled. Standing up to stretch her back, she notices her uncles setting off towards the orchard, and decides it might be time to go home and tend the goats. Only the robin, whose brain has not been chipped, chooses to stay where he is.

Amuse-Bouche

Sherri Turner

'TODAY CHEF IS offering a salad of jambon de campagne, chèvre and grapefruit. Enjoy!'

The pattern on the over-sized plates takes up more space than the food.

'We didn't order this,' he whispers.

'It's extra,' she says. 'Amuse-bouche – an appetiser.'

'Will they charge for it?'

'No.'

'That's all right then.'

The salt and sharp hit her tongue and she is in Sicily. He is naked on the sand beside her, feeding her segments of red orange. She can still taste the sea in her mouth and his sweat on her lips. They are similar, but different. Salt is not just salt after all.

'It's nice here, isn't it?' she says.

'A bit poncey. And pricey, too. Fifteen quid for soup?'

'It's my treat.'

'Even so. Fifteen quid!'

'For madam, white asparagus with a quail's egg hollandaise and micro herbs. For sir, velouté of chanterelle with shavings of black truffle.'

'I thought you ordered me mushroom soup,' he says, once the waiter has left.

'That's what that is.'

'Oh. What's with all the shavings of this and micro that?'

'They add to the dish, bring out the flavours.'

'I don't see the point.'

'No.'

It's the small things that make the difference: the look in his eyes, the gossamer touch on an ankle, the kiss in the crook of an elbow. He makes her wait and the waiting is a joy.

'How was the asparagus?'

'Delicious,' she says.

'Chateaubriand for two, with baby herb potatoes. Would madam like her sauce on the side?'

'Thank you.'

'Sir?'

'Is there any gravy?'

'If sir would like gravy I can have chef make some.'

'Oh, never mind. No sauce, thanks.'

On the side. Such a dismissive term for something so enhancing, so astonishing, so central. The beef is soft and tender, the potatoes creamy and delicate, but without the sauce they are diminished, unfulfilled. He makes love to her on the beach, on her balcony, in the orange grove. They make gentle love, urgent love, lazy love.

'That was good. Can't beat meat and potatoes.' He rubs his stomach, satisfied.

'You should have tried the sauce.'

'Would madam like dessert? Coffee?'

'Just an espresso.'

'Sir?'

'Do you do apple pie?'

'We have tarte tatin.'

'That's almost the same,' she says.

'I'll have that then.'

The coffee is strong and bitter. It wipes the other flavours from her mouth. He eats the tarte in three bites. She can see its sweetness and wishes she had ordered it. No. Better to end it this way.

'Could we have the bill, please?'

It costs more than she expected, it always does. She doesn't mind.

'I'm glad you're home,' he says. 'I missed you.'

'It's only once a year.' She hesitates. 'Maybe you could come next time.'

'I don't like all that foreign food,' he says. 'Anyway, we both need our space.'

And he smiles and remembers tinned soup, meat and potatoes, apple pie and rumpled sheets in an Eastbourne guesthouse.

About the Authors

JENNIFER FALKNER

Jennifer Falkner (she/her) lives in Ottawa, Canada, on the traditional, unceded territory of the Algonquin Anishinaabeg First Nation. Her work has appeared in numerous publications, both in print and online. In 2021, she won the Little Bird writing contest in 2021, judged by Sheena Kamal. Her short story, *The Inventory*, was nominated by *Agnes and True* for the 2019 Journey Prize. In 2018 she was awarded first and second place in the HWA/Dorothy Dunnett short story competition. She has a novella (Fish Gotta Swim Editions) and a short story collection (Invisible Publishing) forthcoming.

HOLLY BARRATT

Holly Barratt lives in Cardiff, Wales. She writes short stories in many genres and is currently editing her first science fiction novel. Previous stories have been published by Wyldblood Press, Leaf Books, Oxford Greats in Flash and the Brick Lane Short Story Competition. She has an MA in Creative Writing from Chichester University. She is inspired by history, folklore, nature, memories and dreams. Writing fights for space in her life alongside a full-time job, cat parenting, and a serious martial arts and yoga habit.

JOHN HOLLAND

John Holland is a short fiction author from Gloucestershire in the UK. He started writing aged 59, and ten years on, has won first prize in short fiction competitions on five occasions, including To Hull And Back in 2018. His work, which is often darkly comic, has been published more than a hundred times in print anthologies and online—including in *The Molotov Cocktail, Truffle Magazine, Spelk, The Phare, Ellipsis Zine, The Cabinet of Heed, Reflex Fiction, Storgy, Riot Act* and NFFD. John also runs the twice-yearly event Stroud Short Stories. Website www.johnhollandwrites.com

Twitter @JohnHol88897218.

JANE FRASER

Jane Fraser lives, works and writes in the Gower peninsula, south Wales. Her first collection of short fiction, *The South Westerlies* was published by SALT in 2019. Her debut novel, *Advent* was published in January 2021 by HONNO, the UK's longest-standing independent women's press. In 2017 she was a finalist in the Manchester Fiction Prize and in 2018 a prize winner in the Fish Memoir Prize. She is an alumni of Swansea University with an MA (distinction) and PhD in Creative Writing. She was a Hay Festival Writer at Work in 2018 and 2019.She is grandmother to Megan, Florence and Alice.

A full bio at www.janefraserwriter.com.

Represented by Literary Agent, Gaia Banks, at Sheil Land Literary Associates www.sheilland.com.

CORRINA O'BIERNE

Corrina is a writer/playwright based in Brighton. She recently completed a writers attachment programme in association with Oxford Playhouse. Her play 'Come on in, we're open' was shortlisted for the Kenneth Branagh award for new drama writing (2017). Her short stories have been published by Bridport Prize and literary magazines and she was shortlisted in the Fish Publishing Short Story Award (2020).

ALI MCGRANE

Ali McGrane lives and writes between the sea and the moor, in the south west UK. Her stories can be found in online litmags, including Ellipsis Zine, FlashBack Fiction, Janus Literary and Splonk. Her work has been longlisted for the Fish Flash Fiction Prize, shortlisted for the Bath Flash Fiction Award, and received nominations for Best of the Net and Best Microfictions. Her Bath shortlisted novella-in-flash, *The Listening Project*, will be published in 2021 by Ad Hoc Fiction.

NASTASYA PARKER

Nastasya Parker's contemporary literary fiction has appeared in two Bristol Short Story Prize anthologies, Stroud Short Story events, Perhappened magazine, and The Phare. After growing up in the United States, she now lives in Gloucestershire, UK. She's currently editing her irreverent novel giving Eve's perspective on the creation myth, and blogging about the random stories we find in daily life, at nastasyaparker.com.

RHYS TIMSON

Rhys Timson has had stories published by Litro, The London Magazine, Bandit Fiction, Popshot, 3:AM, Structo, Lighthouse and other journals. His work has been performed at Liars' League and appeared in previous Retreat West anthologies.

HENRY HEFFER

Longtime advocate of the 'unpublishable' genre, Henry has written five novels, two novellas, one screenplay and a whole host of short stories, the manuscripts of which are currently being used to prop up a 1996 Skoda Octavia. Henry dreams of one day selling a manuscript so he can finally give up writing altogether and follow his true passion: embroidering birds of paradise into aeroplane neck pillows.

If you enjoyed his story and wish to purchase a neck

pillow, please visit Henry's website which will be back up and running when he remembers where he put it.

EMILY HARRISON

Emily talks to herself at night, when all the shadows in her room start to move. She has had work published with X-R-A-Y Literary Magazine, Ellipsis Zine, Barren Magazine, STORGY Magazine, The Molotov Cocktail, Coffin Bell, Retreat West, Litro, Tiny Molecules and Gone Lawn to name a few. She has been nominated for Best Small Fictions.

JASON JACKSON

Jason Jackson's fiction appears regularly in print and online. Recently his stories have been nominated for the Pushcart Prize as well as appearing in the BIFFY 50 and Best Microfictions. This year, in addition to *Apple-Fall* winning the Retreat West Flash Fiction competition, *What Comes Next*was awarded second place in The Phare's inaugural Writewords competition, and *Next-Door Charlie and Carol in Winter* was shortlisted for the Bath Flash Fiction Award. Jason is also a photographer and his prose/photography piece *The Unit* is published by A3 Press. Jason co-edits of the online magazine Janus Literary.

REBECCA NETLEY

Rebecca Netley is a writer from Berkshire. She writes novels and short fiction. Her new novel, *The Whistling,* a ghost story, comes out in October 2021 with Penguin Michael Joseph. She has also won prizes and listed for short fiction.

E.E. RHODES

E. E. Rhodes is an archaeologist who lives in Worcestershire where she is part of the ACE-funded Writing West Midlands Room 204 programme. She's won or placed in more than forty competitions with both prose and poetry, and her work features in a range of journals, magazines, and anthologies. She's a columnist for Spelt Magazine writing about rural issues and a reader for Twin Pies Literary.

MORGAN QUINN

Morgan lives, writes and teaches in North West England. She started writing in June 2020 and fell in love with flash fiction for its wonderful breadth, and glorious brevity. Her stories have recently won third prize at Flash 500, and 4th prize at Reflex Fiction. She also has flash fiction published or forthcoming—online and in anthologies— with Crow and Crosskeys, Funny Pearls, FlashBack Fiction, NFFD and Bath Flash Fiction.

RAE COWIE

Rae Cowie's flash fiction has been shortlisted in *Retreat West, Flash 500* and the *Scottish Association of Writers'* competitions, as well as being longlisted for the *Bath Flash Fiction Award,* and published in *Romance Matters* and *Potluck Zine.*

Her short stories have been longlisted by *Fish Publishing* and published in the Scottish Book Trust *'Rebel'* anthology, *The Scottish Field Magazine* and *Northwords Now.* The highlight of her writing career was winning the Romantic Novelists' Association Elizabeth Goudge award.

She writes in rural Aberdeenshire, creating a debut anthology, one flash at a time.

JAN KANEEN

Jan Kaneen has an MA in Creative Writing from the Open University and her writing has won prizes in places like Molotov Cocktail, Bath Flash Fiction, Flash 500 and Fountain Magazine. She's been published widely in print and online in places like Aesthetica, The Fish Anthology and the Dinesh Allirajah Award Anthology. Her debut memoir-in-flash, *The Naming of Bones* is available from Retreat West Books.

CHARLIE SWAILES

Charlie Swailes is a secondary school teacher, living in West Yorkshire with her husband and two small sons. She began sharing her flash fiction in the summer of 2019 and has been fortunate enough to be published by a variety of online publications, include Reflex Fiction, Retreat West and Flash 500, coming second in their quarterly competition. Her stories have also appeared in the 2020 and 2021 National Flash Fiction Day Anthologies. Twitter @CharlieSWrites.

DAN MICKLETHWAITE

Dan Micklethwaite writes stories in a shed in the north of England, some of which have recently featured in Little Blue Marble, Tales from Fiddler's Green, and PodCastle. His debut novel, *The Less than Perfect Legend of Donna Creosote*, was published by Bluemoose Books. Follow him on twitter @Dan_M_writer, and check out danmicklethwaite.co.uk for more information.

PETE BARNES

Writing from his home overlooking the Peak District, Pete Barnes initially focused on sitcom scripts and comedy sketches, but is now a committed short story writer, with a particular fondness for flash fiction. His work has been published in three anthologies so far, and he won second prize in the Swoop Books Creative Writing Competition 2020.

SHERRI TURNER

Sherri Turner has had numerous short stories published in magazines and has won prizes for both poetry and short stories in competitions including the Bristol Prize, the Wells Literary Festival and the Bridport Prize. Her work has appeared in several anthologies and in many places online. She tweets at @STurner4077.

Printed in Great Britain
by Amazon

66454512R00098